Torn
Copyright © 2018 Vivian Rose
ViviRose Publishing
All rights reserved. No part of th in any
form or by any means (electronic ....., including photocopying, record,
or any information storage and retrieval systems, without prior written permission
of the Author. Your support of Author's rights is appreciated. This is a work of
fiction. References may be made to locations and historical events; however,
names, characters, places, and incidents are either the product of the author's
imagination or are used fictitiously. Any resemblance to actual persons (living or
dead), business establishments, events, or locales is entirely coincidental. All
trademarks, service marks, registered trademarks, and registered service marks are
the property of their respective owner.

To David Clybourn

Rest in Peace Uncle. You will be missed.

July 16, 2018

Blurb

Cayla Sherman is distraught over the recent loss of her incredible husband, but before she even has time to fully grieve, she is dealt another harsh blow that almost brings her to her knees. However, Cayla is motivated to "get back up again" in order to weather the storms of deception and destruction.

Maxwell Washington had been best friends with Jonathan Sherman since
childhood. But when his best friend dies, Max is emotionally lost and spent. Somehow Max must pick up the pieces and find Jon's missing wife, Cayla, so that he can keep his promise of watching over her through her sorrow and pain.
Will Cayla and Max find more than friendship? We can only imagine.

Dedication
Lena H.
My Collaborator
My Sister, My Friend, My Muse

Acknowledgments
Lee Summers
Editor

Renee Luke
Cover Designer
Cover Me – Book Covers

Prologue

Cayla Sherman answered the door to the condominium. Standing on the threshold of her door was her mother-in-law, Margaret Sherman, as well as her sisters-in-law, Sherri and Sharon. She frowned, wondering why they had come. They didn't like her and never missed a chance to remind her of that fact. She knew for certain it wasn't to see how she was holding up - even if she *had* just buried her husband a month ago.

"Hello, Mrs. Sherman," Cayla greeted politely.

"Cayla," she said, pushing past her. Her daughters followed behind her in a huff. Cayla closed the door and turned to look at them. They eyed her with distaste which was nothing new. When Jon was alive, they tried to disguise their dislike of her in his presence, but it was obvious that they didn't approve of Jonathan's choice for a wife. Two years after Jon and Cayla met, they said they're *I do's*. She constantly heard from his mother how Jon married beneath him as if she were nothing but mere trash - a gold digger after his money.

"Cayla, we are here to help you move," Mrs. Sherman announced haughtily.

Cayla frowned at her. "Move? I'm not moving."

"Yes, my dear, you are. This was Jonathan's condo, and he is no longer with us. The spell you wove over him is now broken. It died along with him, so pack your bags and get out. Now!" she stated sternly.

"This is my home also, Mrs. Sherman. I've lived..."

"Quiet!" she snapped. "You are no longer welcome in this family and being the executrix of his estate and having possession of his power of attorney, I want you out. This. Moment."

"But I was his wife!" Cayla replied.

"And now you are not. Did you think Jon would leave provisions for you? Well, he did not. I knew the minute he brought you into my home that you were only after his money and anything else you could get your slimy little hands on. When he realized his mistake in marrying you and what kind of person you are, he made sure he left you with nothing but the rags you walked in here with," she said with an evil chuckle.

"I loved Jon very much," Cayla stated.

"Yeah right, you loved Jon's money and prestige," Sherri, the younger sister, said venomously.

Cayla looked from one to the other. She couldn't believe this was happening. She had lost Jon; now, she was losing her home. This had to be some twisted joke because she knew that Jon loved her beyond a shadow of a doubt - unconditionally.

"You can't do this," Cayla declared.

"Oh, but I can. After all, I am his mother, and you are nothing but gutter trash! If you hadn't come into his life, he would still be with us. But noo, you had him rushing home to be with you. Why he would do such a thing is beyond me. Now, because I'm not totally heartless, I have movers waiting downstairs for instructions to clear out the condo. You can then resume your ghetto fabulous life. Heed my warning: if you fight me, I will have the police remove you, and I will press charges to send your little ass to jail. I want you out of our lives forever, and I mean right now!"

"I need time to pack," Cayla cried.

"No, they will do it for you. I suggest you get some clothing and find a place to go. They will be coming up as soon as I instruct them." Margaret paused and looked at the décor of the home. "I should tell them to put all this mess on the curb. Your taste in décor is just like you - horrible, but that's neither here nor there." She waved her hand dismissively. "I was able to rent a storage area for you to place this junk in. The storage is paid up for the year, so that will give you time to find a place. Now, hurry up and get some clothing."

"I'm not leaving until they have packed my stuff. I don't want anything broken."

"Whatever, just get to moving."

Cayla turned to go to the other room.

"Oh and, Cayla, I have taken the BMW you were driving. After all, it was also Jonathan's."

"How am I to get around?"

"That is not my problem; walk, catch a bus or train - I could care less. You do get to leave with more than you had when you came into this marriage. Just be happy I'm letting you take this tacky furniture. I could never get rid of it, even if I said it was free."

"You know what, Mrs. Sherman? That's all right; to hell with you and your despicable daughters. You do what you want."

Cayla grabbed her purse off the credenza and her pouch of important papers out of its drawer then headed for the door. She paused and glanced around the home she and Jon had shared. They had been happy, and this witch couldn't take her memories. Cayla took a deep breath.

"I hope you have a good life, Mrs. Sherman, but you know what they say: what goes around comes around. I heard karma is a bitch!"

Cayla slammed the door behind her. Everything she and Jon owned would soon become nothing more than memories. Tears blinded her as she went down the steps and to her unknown future.

Chapter One

Six months later

Wearily Cayla exited the employee entrance of the Ritz-Carlton Hotel in the Buckhead Area of Atlanta and entered the alley. She paused a moment, leaned against the brick building, and exhaled. It had to be one of the hottest days of July, she thought, as she pushed her bone-tired body from the wall. The humidity was suffocating even though it was past midnight. She looked down the long alley and wondered if she was going to make it to the bus stop without passing out. She let out an exhausted sigh. Oh, well. She finally willed herself to start moving. For the past three months, she'd worked overtime and sometimes she would pull a double. She wasn't sure how long she would be able to continue like this, but her needs were greater than her desires. She had to save money so she could find a better place to live. She ran a shaky hand over her long hair tucked into a ponytail and began to walk. When she reached the end of the alley, she stopped again, leaning against the building to rest and catch her breath.

Her eyes shut briefly. "Oh, Jonathan, I miss you so much. I wish you were here to hold me and assure me that everything was going to be alright. God, baby, I would give anything, anything, for just a minute with you," she spoke softly as tears leaked down her cheeks. "Okay, Cayla, you've got to put on your big girl panties and suck it up. You have to keep on moving." Filling her lungs with more air and exhaling, she took the steps needed to get her to her destination.

Daily living had become a struggle for her ever since Mrs. Sherman and her evil daughters came and put her out of the home she and Jonathan shared. Luckily, she was able to find a job at the Ritz as a room attendant; however, finding a small efficiency apartment in Atlanta's projects that she could afford hadn't been an easy feat.

Maxwell Washington stood outside the Ritz with his hands pushed into his pockets. He had to get some much-needed air from those stuffy, superficial people inside. It didn't matter how hot it was outside, he had to get away before he said something he would later regret. He was tired of those condescending, haughty people he had to deal with while they looked down their nose at others. He sighed. He missed his best friend, his brother – Jon. If Jon were here, they would find something humorous about the people that they called their peers and constituents.

Jonathan Sherman had been from one of Atlanta's wealthiest African-American families, and he had also been his business partner in their successful architectural firm. Six months ago, he had been killed in a car accident by a drunk driver while on his way home to his wife, Cayla. Maxwell had just spoken to Jon, who told him he had some good news but was anxious to get home to his wife. Then the news of his death was the last Maxwell had heard about his friend.

He and Jonathan Sherman had been best friends since they were young boys, and when Jon tragically died, a part of Maxwell died along with him. He often wondered how Jon's wife, Cayla, was doing. He remembered how devastated and inconsolable she was at Jon's funeral. Since his best friend was gone, he felt obligated to look out for her, but a month after Jon was buried, she disappeared - whereabouts unknown. He went to Jon's mother and asked if she had heard from Cayla. Mrs. Sherman looked at him as if he had cursed at her, asking him how she would know. She probably *didn't* know. Jon's mother and sisters didn't care for or approve of Jon's wife. They told anyone who would listen that she was from the wrong side of the tracks and didn't deserve Jon. Max just left it alone and hoped she was alright. However, it didn't stop him from wondering about her and how she was.

He and Jon had just left each other the night he had been killed. Max will never forget the pure joy and happiness on Jon's face whenever he saw Jon and Cayla together.

Jon loved Cayla with his whole being; she was his life, and Max never saw two people more in love. Cayla was a good person, and she adored Jon. They were perfect together. The thought caused Maxwell to wonder if there was a woman out there that he would want to take those future steps with. Maxwell smiled, recalling when Jon met Cayla for the first time.

Cayla worked at the concession stand at the Georgia Dome. They were at the Dome to see the Atlanta Buetos play. Jon was smitten at first sight, and Max had to admit Cayla was beautiful. At first, Cayla ignored Jon. Every time some event was at the Dome, Jon would drag him along. It didn't matter what the event was, Jon was there. After a couple of months, she agreed to go out with him. They dated a year before Jon literally swept Cayla off her feet to Las Vegas, where they exchanged vows. Max was happy for his friend because he knew Cayla and Jon loved each other. Jon's mother and sisters were not happy about the union, and behind his back, they were downright cruel to Cayla. She took their verbal abuse in stride because Jon loved his mother and sisters. She had once told Max that she loved Jon enough to endure whatever they did or said to her. Max sighed and leaned against the wall. He needed to get back inside. If this wasn't business, he would have never attended.

Cayla was exhausted, but she had to keep pushing on and ignore the perspiration running down the side of her face as she made her way to the bus stop bench. If she were lucky, she wouldn't have long to wait for the bus, then she would have to walk a couple of blocks from the bus stop to her apartment. She prayed for strength.

Max couldn't help but notice the woman walking slowly past him. Her head rose briefly. She glanced at him, but she didn't even see him.

Max stared at the woman in disbelief as recognition dawned. This couldn't be the beautiful woman Jon married two and a half years ago. Her once lustrous hair was dull, lifeless, and pulled back into a frazzled ponytail. The flawless nutmeg face was drawn and ashen; her once clear brown eyes, dull and languid. Back then her pretty face was full and happy but was now thin and somber. Max's eyes trailed down her body. Her rounded belly protruded like a round ball in front of her. Cayla was pregnant. How could that be? The last time he saw Cayla was at Jon's funeral. He didn't get to talk to her then. Having taken Jon's death extremely hard, he could barely hold himself together. The last time he spoke to Jon, his best friend said he had some good news for Max. So this was the good news Jon said he would tell him about later because he had needed to get home to his wife. Jon had been overjoyed. Yes, this explained it all.

Max moved from the wall. He couldn't believe the transformation from a once-happy wife to this withdrawn and sickly looking young woman - and she was pregnant. Max quickly calculated, and if he was correct, Cayla was carrying Jon's child.

"Cayla!" he called, following behind her. She stopped and turned; instant recognition was in her eyes.

"Maxwell? Hello," she said softly.

Max frowned at her. She looked so tired.

"How are you?" she asked politely.

"Cayla," he repeated her name. His eyes dropped to her belly. "Are you carrying Jon's child?" he asked.

Cayla's eyes met his, and her eyebrows dipped. "Don't worry about it," she said and started to move away.

Max watched as she walked away. He was confused.

"Cayla, wait!" he called from behind her.

She ignored him and kept walking.

Max caught up with her and grabbed her arm. Cayla snatched away.

"What do you want?" she hissed as she looked up into his eyes.

"I've been trying to find you. Where have you been?" Max asked her.

It was her turn to look confused. "Why?" she asked.

"I wanted to know how you were, but Mrs. Sherman said you moved out a month after Jon died."

Max didn't miss the tension in her body at the mention of her former mother-in-law's name.

"Yes, well I didn't have much choice, now did I?" she replied tersely.

Max looked her, bewildered. "What do you mean?"

"Nothing, Maxwell. It was good seeing you," she stated then turned and continued up the sidewalk.

"Cayla," Max called again, going to her. She stopped.

"Maxwell, I have to catch the next bus, and right now I'm just too tired to talk."

"Well, can I wait with you?" he asked gently.

"Suit yourself," she said, shrugging and moving away.

Maxwell sat beside her on the bus stop bench, trying desperately not to stare at her. "How are you?" Max asked with concern in his voice.

Cayla looked over at him, hearing his concern. Why would he care, she wondered? Wasn't he one of them?

"We are just fine, Maxwell," she replied, turning her face away.

"Cayla, I have to ask. Is that Jon's child?"

Cayla looked over at him. "Would you believe me if I said yes?" she countered.

"Of course I would," Max said indignantly.

She didn't believe that, so she didn't comment. It didn't matter what Max thought, she decided.

"You don't look well, Cayla. Have you been taking care of yourself?"

Cayla looked over at him. At one time, she really liked Maxwell Washington. He had always been so kind to her, but right now she didn't want to talk to him.

"I'm fine."

Max looked at her closely. He could see the perspiration on her brow and upper lip. It was a hot night but not that hot. He watched as her eyes closed for the briefest minute and then opened. He heard her grunt, and she squeezed her eyes shut again.

"Cayla, I don't think you're well at all," Max stated.

Her eyes opened slowly, and her head turned to him.

"I'm fine, Maxwell, really - just tired," she tried to assure him. It was just the hot weather that was getting to her.

"No, Cayla, you're not well. I can see it on your face." Max reached over and placed the back of his hand on her forehead. She was ashen, cool, and clammy.

"Do you feel lightheaded?"

"It's just the heat, Maxwell. I'm fine," she insisted. Cayla looked past him. Finally, her bus was coming. She rose to her feet; Max rose with her.

"Maybe I ought to take you to the hospital," he stated to her.

"No, I'm fine."

"Cayla, please... just to be safe. Think about Jon's child," he stated firmly.

Cayla stared at Max, surprise registering in her dull brown eyes. "How do you know this is Jon's child?" she asked skeptically.

"Please, Cayla, just to be on the safe side."

Cayla shook her head. "Max, I can't afford an emergency room bill. I..."

"What? Look, don't worry about that now; just come with me, Cayla, please?" Cayla sighed. "Okay, Maxwell."

"Can you make it to the valet booth?" he asked, holding her arm.

"I guess so," she said and took a step. Her knees buckled, but Maxwell caught her before she fell to her knees. "Just sit here, Cayla. I'll be right back," he said while rushing away.

Cayla sat. The bus pulled up, and she waved him away. She closed her eyes for a minute to regroup. She knew she would need all of her energy to deal with Maxwell and all of the questions he was bound to ask. When her eyes opened, Max was helping her to her feet. He opened the door to his Mercedes and helped her inside the car. Cayla let her head fall back as he put the seat belt across her belly. Max rushed to the driver's side of the car and took off. He glanced over at Cayla; her eyes remained closed.

"Cay, you still with me?" he asked with concern while touching her clammy skin. She nodded, not bothering to open her eyes.

Ten minutes later, Max was pulling up to the hospital ER entrance. He rushed around to open the door and help Cayla out the car. Looking up, Cayla placed her hand in his as he helped her rise. Her vision suddenly blurred and then she passed out. Max caught her in his arms, lifted her, and rushed into the hospital. The nurse behind the desk rushed to him. "Let's take her to the back," she told him. Max followed.

"What happened?" she asked as he followed her. "Lay her here," the nurse instructed.

"I was helping her from the car, and she just passed out."

"Doctor!" the nurse called.

Max stepped around her bed. The doctor started examining her.

"How many months is she, sir?" the doctor asked Max.

"I think about six or seven months."

"She's very clammy. Has this happened before?"

"I don't know; she's my friend's wife. I just happened to see her, and she didn't look well. I convinced her to come here. What's wrong with her?" Max asked worriedly.

"Take him outside, Nurse, and get her information while I examine her," the doctor told the nurse. Max hesitated for a minute. "She's in good hand with Dr. Bryant. He's an obstetrician, the best in the state," the nurse reassured him after seeing the concern in his eyes. Max followed the nurse out.

The nurse sat across from him in the waiting area, with a clipboard in hand to take the patient's information.

"Name?"

"Cayla Sherman."

"Age?"

"I think she's twenty-five."

"You say she's six or seven months?"

"Yes, I think so."

"Married?"

"No, widowed." The nurse looked up at him.

"Family?"

"None that I know of."

"Can I put you down as *next of kin* then?"

"Yes, Maxwell Washington."

"Insurance?"

"I don't know. I'll take care of her medical costs." The nurse looked up at him curiously. Max noticed.

"She was married to my best friend; he was killed in a car accident six months ago."

The nurse nodded with sympathy in her eyes. "Sign by the *X,* Mr. Washington. The doctor should be out soon to talk with you," she said, handing him the clipboard for his signature.

Max sat back in the chair, wondering what had happened to Cayla? She should be living very comfortably now. Jon left her his entire estate. He knew because he witnessed the signing of the will and all his other financial transactions. He had insurance and stocks - not only in their company but also in others. Something wasn't right, and he meant to find out what had happened to her. Catching a bus! Jon had left Cayla all five of his automobiles. He even had a trust established for any future children they would have. He knew it; he was there. Cayla and the child were set for life. So why is she walking the street of Atlanta this late at night?

"Mr. Washington," the doctor said, approaching him. Max rose.

"Who is her primary care doctor?"

"I don't know. Is she alright?"

"Well no, she's not. I just got her test results a few moments ago. Thank goodness you brought her in when you did. She has signs of hypoglycemia, which means she has an abnormally low blood sugar level. Do you know if she is a diabetic?"

"I don't think so. Is Cayla awake?"

"Yes, you can come with me. She's very frightened, and she wants to leave the hospital; however, she has to stay with us for at least a couple of days until we can get her blood sugar level up. It's important for the welfare of the child and mother."

"Of course; I will talk to her." Max followed Dr. Bryant to the examining room.

"Cayla," Max said softly after coming in with the doctor.

"Max, I can't stay here," she sounded panicked and scared.

"Cay, listen to the doctor, please. It's important for you and the baby."

The doctor went to the other side of the bed.

"Mrs. Sherman, you have a case of hypoglycemia, which means your blood sugar is low. Are you a diabetic?"

"No."

"Good."

"Have you been under a lot of stress lately?"

Cayla stared, frowning at the doctor. She didn't want him to know just how much, especially with Max standing there.

"Mrs. Sherman?"

She shrugged. "I guess. I've been working a lot of overtime lately," she stated. "I thought I was just overheated and a little tired."

"Where do you work?"

"I'm a room attendant at the Ritz."

The doctor shook his head. "And you are working overtime in your condition? Who is your primary doctor?" Cayla didn't answer right away.

"You are seeing an obstetrician, aren't you, Mrs. Sherman?"

"I guess. I go to the clinic in downtown Atlanta. I don't have just one doctor. I see whoever is available when I have my appointments."

Dr. Bryant looked back at Max. Cayla noticed the exchange.

"What?" she said, looking at the doctor.

"That's not the most reliable place for you to be - not with your condition. Did your physician approve of your doing extra work?"

"He said if I feel up to it, it was alright."

"Well, Mrs. Sherman, you're not up to it. You have to stay off your feet if you want to carry the baby to full term and deliver a healthy baby. Now, I think you're about six months, right?"

Cayla nodded with tears filling her eyes. She looked over at Max.

"You don't understand. I have to work, or I can't feed this baby when it's born."

"You don't have any family that could help you?"

She shook her head, tears rolling down her face.

"Mrs. Sherman, you are under a lot of stress. I think that is the cause of your low blood sugar. Now I'm going to have to keep you and monitor you and the child for a couple of days."

"Can you take me to City hospital? At least there I can get charity care. I can't afford this hospital."

"No, Mrs. Sherman."

"Why?"

"Because you are now my patient, and I want to ensure you are well cared for at my hospital."

"How much do you charge?"

"Cayla, don't worry about that right now," Max replied to her.

"That's right. Now, I'm going to have you moved to a room and give you something so you can rest, which is what you need right now. Have you had an ultrasound?"

"No, that's extra at the clinic."

"Okay, I'm scheduling you for an ultrasound tomorrow. Mr. Washington, can you stay for a while so we can get her admitted?"

"Certainly. I'll take care of everything, Dr. Bryant. Anything she needs. I want her in a private room also."

The doctor nodded, leaving them alone.

Cayla let her head fall back, and tears leaked from her tightly shut eyes.

Max went to stand beside the bed. "Cayla, don't worry about anything. I'll take care of everything. I just don't understand what happened to you. You shouldn't be struggling like this, let alone working as a room attendant."

Cayla's eyes opened, and she stared at him in disbelief.

"How else was I going to take care of this child, Max? I had to find a job."

"What about...?" Max stopped. Now was not the time. He would talk to her about this when she was stronger.

"Cayla, just get better; we'll work everything out, I promise. Jon was my best friend, and we were closer than brothers. If I only knew," he said in a sad tone.

The nurse came in. "The orderlies will be in to move you to your room in a few minutes, Mrs. Sherman. Dr. Bryant wants you to get plenty of rest. Have you eaten today?"

"No, I had some crackers at about five o'clock."

"Dr. Bryant didn't think so. We are going to send something to eat up to you when you get settled, then we will give you something so you can rest." Cayla nodded.

She lay back quietly. Max stood alongside her, looking at her. She looked at Max.

"I miss him so much, Maxwell," she admitted.

"Me too." Max took her hand in his.

"Cayla, let me help you. Jon was my friend, and I just can't accept seeing you alone and struggling. I promise you this: I'm going to find out what happened to you after Jon died, whether you want to divulge the answers or not. I will hound you until you relent," he smiled, showing his dimples."

The orderlies came in and moved Cayla upstairs, with Max following behind them.

Once she was settled in, a tray with a sandwich and bowl of soup was brought to her. Max sat in the only available chair in the room, watching as she ate. She was eating as if she hadn't eaten in a while.

"Cayla, are you eating well?"

"I eat at work most times. Why?"

"You seem hungry." She didn't respond to that.

"Max, can you go to my apartment to get me some things?"

"Sure, what do you need?"

"On the far wall is a dresser. I need some underwear, a nightgown, and some clothes. Everything is in that dresser. It doesn't matter what you pick; anything will be fine."

"Keys?"

"Oh, in my uniform pocket over there," she said, pointing.

"Where do you live?"

"560 College St, Apt 30C, downtown," she told him. Max frowned. He knew that area and knew it was not the safest place to live, but he didn't comment. The nurse came back in to administer a shot that would help her sleep.

"Max, thank you so much," she said before her eyes closed. It wasn't long before Cayla was sound asleep and softly snoring.

Chapter Two

The next morning, Max went to Cayla's apartment. He couldn't believe what he saw. Her place was clean, but it was nothing more than an efficiency apartment. The room had a twin-size bed and a hot plate. Beside it was a box with different types of canned soup, a small saucepan, and a bowl with a spoon in it. Goodness, was this all she lived off, he wondered? A 13-inch television sat on a scratched-up TV stand; there was a bedside table with a lamp; and, the dresser stood on the far wall. The bathroom was nothing but a toilet and a small shower stall. The room was dark and very dank. He even saw a couple of roaches crawling up the wall. Now he was angry and pissed as all get out.

"What happened to you, Cayla?" Max asked out loud while shaking his head.

Jonathan would not want this for the woman he loved or his child. He left her set for life. He couldn't allow her to continue living in this condition. There was no way in hell he was leaving her here in this roach-infested dump. She would be in the hospital for a couple of days, so that would give him time to find a place for her. He would have to enlist his mother's help in purchasing her some decent clothes because there was no way he was taking any of these things with him. Max went through the drawers looking for any papers he thought she would need. He found a folder that said *important papers*. When he left the room, that was all he had in his hand.

Max then went to the Ritz Carlton Human Resources department to speak to her employer.

"Mr. Assaulta, I'm Maxwell Washington, a friend of Cayla Sherman," Max introduced himself.

"Please have a seat," Mr. Assaulta invited. "Is Cayla alright? She didn't come in this morning."

"She's in the hospital."

"I'm sorry to hear that. Is she going to be alright?"

"She'll be fine. I just wanted to let you know she will not be returning. The doctor has her on complete bed rest until after her baby is born," Max informed him.

"Will she be returning afterward?"

"I doubt it."

"Cayla's a great person and a model employee. If there is anything I can do for her, please tell her to give me a call, Mr. Washington."

"Thank you, I'll tell her." Max rose and shook his hand.

Max left the Ritz and went to his mother's house. Harriett Washington, a statuesque woman, opened the door to her son. She smiled at him with the same dimples winking in her cheeks. She kissed him on both cheeks in greeting.

"Good morning, my son. What brings you here so early?"

"Mom, I need your help, and I need some answers."

"Come on in. I'm making coffee; have a cup while we talk."

Max followed his mother to the kitchen. He and his mother had always had a very close relationship. After his father passed away five years ago, he made it a habit of stopping in daily to see her. Although she had a full life with her charities and women's clubs, he still worried about her.

"Sit down, Son." Max sat at the table while his mother poured him a cup of black coffee.

"Hungry, baby?"

"I'm fine."

Harriett sat across from her son and didn't miss the strain of worry on his handsome face.

"Okay, tell Mama what's going on?"

"Do you remember Jon's wife, Cayla?"

"Oh yes, lovely person. I haven't seen her since Jon's funeral."

"Well, I ran into her last night in front of the Ritz. Cayla is six months pregnant with Jon's child and not too well. I had to rush her to the hospital. They had to keep her. They said her blood sugar levels were very low."

"Really? I didn't know. I'm really sorry to hear that. Will she be okay?"

"She needs rest, the doctor said. Mom, what happened to her? I mean, after Jon died, she moved out of their condo. She's now living in downtown Atlanta in this roach-infested apartment right behind College Park, and she's working as a room attendant at the Ritz. I know Jon left her well situated. I just don't understand why she's so destitute. Have you heard *anything* about her?"

"I asked Margaret about her once at church. She said she took care of Cayla. I just assumed by what she said that she helped her through that drastic time period, but I should have known better," his mother supplied. "I know Margaret and her horrible daughters never liked Cayla, and they never had anything kind to say about her. I also know that when Jon married her, Margaret told anyone who would listen that she knew Cayla married Jon for his money."

"Mom, Mrs. Sherman is doing nothing for Cayla. I don't even think she's eating regularly."

Harriett shook her head sadly. "So, what do you need me to do?"

"First, she needs some clothes taken to the hospital, along with toiletries, nightgowns, and other women's things. I didn't take anything from the apartment she lived in, so spare no expense in getting what she needs for the interim as well as for when she's released. Just let me know the cost or take one of my cards."

"Okay, Max, I'll take care of that for you. Now, what else?"

"I need you to find out what happened to Cayla. She's not going to tell me anything, and I really don't want to push too hard unless that's my only alternative.

Maybe if you talk to Mrs. Sherman, she might tell you something. For now, don't talk to her about the baby. I have a feeling Cayla never mentioned it to Mrs. Sherman."

"You're probably right. I'll stop by Margaret's this afternoon," his mother agreed.

"Thanks, Mom. Right now I'm going to see about a place for Cayla to live. I saw this small bungalow about three miles from here. The realtor is going to meet me at ten. I have to go because I only have a couple of days to get all of this settled while Cayla's in the hospital."

Harriett smiled at her son. He is such a giving person. The woman that snatches him up will be the luckiest woman in the world.

"Meet me here in two hours. I'll have everything she needs while she's in the hospital. How pregnant is she?"

"She's six months."

Harriett nodded. "Okay, Son, I'll see you in a few hours," she said and kissed her son's cheek. "You're a good man, Maxwell," she added, smiling.

He smiled. "Thanks, Mom."

The small stone-stucco cottage with its gleaming copper bay roof and arched Merbau-wood door would be perfect for Cayla and the baby. Max met the realtor at the scheduled time for the showing of the cottage. The layout was a nice one: kitchen with a breakfast nook connecting to the great room on one side; the living and dining rooms on the other; and half bath near the living room. The rooms were lined with an overabundance of windows, giving the room a bright, airy appeal. The garage was situated on the west side of the cottage, and there was a nice laundry room. Max followed the realtor as she spoke. The master bedroom had a large sitting area; Cayla could use that as the baby's nursery for the time being. Another bedroom and half bath were next door. Max liked the house, and he thought Cayla would like it as well. There was a large open space above the lower floor that could be used as storage. Being an architect, he had an eye for house structure. The structure was sound, and the house was in excellent condition.

"Well, Mr. Washington?" the realtor said, looking at him as he surveyed the house.

He nodded, deep in thought. "I'll take it on one condition," Max said as he looked into the greedy eyes of the realtor.

The realtor frowned. "And that is?"

"That the transaction has to be completed in two days. If you can't accomplish that, I will find a realtor who can," Max stated sternly.

"Two days, Mr. Washington?" the realtor questioned with a frown. "There's the paperwork, the closing, credit checks, and inspectors. You understand buying a house takes time."

"Fine. Thank you then." Max turned to leave.

The realtor started to panic. "Mr. Washington, I really want to sell you this house. I just don't know if I can have everything complete in two days," she admitted honestly.

Max looked at the middle-aged woman that had spoken so eloquently while trying to convince him this house was for him. The woman was now buckling under a little pressure.

Max wanted the house. It was perfect for Cayla and the baby.

"Well, Ms. Thompson, how about if I tell you that I will double your commission if you can have this house ready to move into in two days?"

Ms. Thompson's eyes widened. "Do you know how much this house is?" she asked, stunned.

"No, I don't."

"Three hundred and fifty thousand."

"So that means you will do very well to sell me this house. So, Ms. Thompson, are you up for the challenge?" Max said, challenging her.

Ms. Thompson looked at him. He didn't flinch when she quoted the price to him.

"Okay, Mr. Washington, this home will be yours in two days," she said, extending her hand and smiling.

"Good," Max said, handing her his business card. "Call me for anything you need. I can have a cashier's check delivered to your office within the hour." Max turned to leave.

"Mr. Washington, do you mean for the full amount of the purchase?" she asked.

"Of course. Just call my office and let my assistant know whatever additional monies are needed, plus your doubled commission." Max opened the front door to the house. Before he left, he turned to look at Ms. Thompson, who had a stunned expression on her face.

"Ms. Thompson, might I suggest you get started?" he said, smiling.

"Of course, Mr. Washington," she stammered and followed behind him.

Max got into his car. Ms. Thompson watched as he pulled out of the driveway with his phone piece to his ear. She turned and looked back at the house, grinning. Mr. Washington had just made her day, and she vowed the house would be ready for him to move into in two days. "Wow, what a man. Ump, ump, ump, if only…"

*****

Cayla lay in the hospital bed, contemplating her next move. The nurse came in with her breakfast and placed the tray on the table.

"How are you feeling today, Mrs. Sherman?"

"Rested," Cayla said with a small smile.

"Good, Dr. Bryant will be glad to hear that."

"How long will I be here?" Cayla asked.

"At least a couple of days. Dr. Bryant wants to make sure you and the baby are healthy before he releases you."

Cayla nodded.

"Is it possible that I can use the phone? I need to call my job."

"That's your phone there. Mr. Washington left instructions to supply anything you need."

"Thank you."

"Now, Mrs. Sherman, eat your breakfast, and I will be back to help you take a shower," the nurse said as she exited the room.

Cayla lifted the cover off the plates of food, realizing she was hungry. She hadn't really had a real meal in a while. She usually ate what she could heat up on her small hot plate in her apartment. So, Cayla attacked the food with vigor as she didn't know when she would enjoy another good meal like this again. After she finished her meal, she called her job.

"Mr. Assaulta, this is Cayla Sherman," she said into the receiver.

"Oh, Cayla, I'm sorry. I heard you were in the hospital. How are you?"

"You heard?"

"Yes, a Mr. Washington stopped by. He told me you had to stop working for a while."

"Mr. Assaulta, I'll be back."

"Cayla, just take care of yourself and the baby. If you need anything, just give me a call. Please don't hesitate to call."

Cayla took a resigned breath. "Thank you, Mr. Assaulta," she said before hanging up the phone.

Why was Maxwell doing this? What did he expect to gain, Cayla wondered? She didn't want his pity or his handouts. She wanted to be as far away from anything that reminded her of Jonathan's society friends and family. She knew when she married Jon that she could never be fully accepted in his circle of friends, not that she cared. She loved Jonathan, not the lifestyle he was raised in. Now all she wanted to do was have her baby, finish her degree in interior design, and open a firm. Jonathan had encouraged her to pursue her dreams, promising her his full support and the necessary funds to start her own business. However, that dream went up in a puff of smoke. After she was put out of Jon's condo, she had to work a full-time job just to keep a roof over her and the baby's head. She was resilient, though. She knew after the baby came she would bounce back, even if she had to work three jobs to make sure her baby was well taken care of. Nothing or no one would stop her or get in her way.

"Oh, Mrs. Sherman, you were very hungry. That's good," the nurse said, coming into the room.

"Now are you ready for a bath?"

"Yes, but I have nothing to put on."

"Mr. Washington called. He said he was bringing a few things for you. For the time being, you can wear a hospital gown."

Cayla nodded and let the nurse help her out of bed.

Max returned to his mother's house to pick up the items for Cayla. His mother had purchased everything Cayla would need and more.

"Max, I'm going to meet with Margaret over lunch this afternoon. I'll find out what happened to Cayla," she informed him. "I just hope I don't have to lay hands on her if she has done something crazy."

Max had known Mrs. Sherman since he was very young when he and Jon became best friends. Max guessed he ought to consider himself lucky that he was even allowed to be friends with Jon. Mrs. Sherman didn't associate with anyone who had nothing, and she instilled that into her daughters. Thank God Jon was nothing like his mother and siblings. The Washingtons, Max's family, were wealthy also; more so than the Shermans, so he was accepted by Jon's family.

Max's mother told him one time that Margaret became a snob after she married into the Sherman family. She had nothing before she met Jon's father, so to protect her assets, anyone with nothing was a threat to her. She thought the less fortunate, or in her terms "poor people," would take all she had. She was like a vicious dog when it came to the lifestyle she had become accustomed to.

"Thanks, Mom," he said, taking the small suitcase from her.

"Did you find a place for her?" Harriett Washington asked.

"Yes, it should be ready by the time she's released. I just need to get it furnished." Max paused, thinking. "Maybe Cayla will want to do that herself. I remember Jon saying she was going to school to get her BA in interior design and is very good at it. She decorated their home. I remember going to their condo, and the place was beautiful. She did everything from the painting of the walls to the polishing of the wood floors."

Harriett smiled at her son. "You like Cayla," his mother commented.

"Yes, Mom, I do. She loved Jon very much. I still can't believe he's gone. I never saw two people more in love. If I ever marry, I would want to have that kind of relationship. Cayla is a good person."

"I always thought she was perfectly lovely, but Margaret continued to demean her character to anyone that would listen."

"Yeah, I know. I remember Jon told me he was tired of hearing his mother and sisters degrade his wife, so he gave his mother an ultimatum. He told her if she couldn't learn to accept his wife, he would leave the family. It worked. Mrs. Sherman stopped saying things about Cayla after that, at least not to him."

Harriett sighed. "Well, she has a friend in you, Son, and I think it's wonderful you are helping her."

"How can I not, Mom? Jon was my best friend. I loved him. Thanks again, Mom. I have to get back to the hospital and talk to Cayla. I hope I can convince her to let me help her. She's a very proud woman."

"Okay, Son, anytime. If you need me to talk to her, I will," Mrs. Washington offered. Max kissed his mother's cheek and left.

Max eased open the door to Cayla's room and found her still sleeping. He entered the room, set the bag down, and went to the side of the bed. He looked down at her and smiled sadly. She still did not stir. The dark circles under her eyes had not diminished, and her face was still gaunt and drawn.

"What happened to you, baby doll? I will get my answers real soon." *I promise you, Jon. I will take care of her just how you would have,* Max vowed to himself. Max sat in the chair by the window, waiting for her to awake. He stretched his long legs out in front of him and closed his eyes. He was tired. He didn't sleep well last night. When he finally fell asleep, he dreamt about Jon. That was the first time he'd dreamt of him since his death six months ago. Jon came to him and told him to take care of Cayla and his son. He'd waken up and couldn't go back to sleep. In the dream, Jon said *his son.* If he believed dreams talked to people, he would believe what Jon said, but he didn't believe in that kind of thing.

Cayla stretched, opening her eyes. She saw Max napping in the chair across the room. How long had he been there, she wondered? She sat up in the bed and looked at Max thoroughly.

Max was a very handsome man. Where Jon was more of a honey color, Max was just a shade darker. His handsome face was kindled with a sort of passionate beauty. He had a generous mouth, an aquiline nose, and dark eyes that spoke of kindness in volumes. His wavy black hair was neat and closely cropped. However, his best asset was his deep bass voice. She also knew he was determined and strong in his personality; not a man people would want to go up against. Jon was the same way. Max was always neat in appearance. Even when he was in sweats or ratty jeans when he and Jon went to the gym or played basketball in the park, he still looked good.

She remembered how formidable Max and Jon were whenever they were together. Both men were tall and muscular, in great physical shape for thirty-year-old men. She didn't miss the many time's women's heads would turn whenever they walked into a room.

Jon was the love of her life. She would never love that way again; not that she wanted to. Jon gave her all the love he had, and she gave him all she had in return. That kind of love only happened once in a lifetime. Cayla felt the ever-flowing tears fill her eyes again, and she often wondered if she would ever get over this grief in her heart. Would she be able to live again? Jon would want her to for both their sakes. She sighed and moved to get out of the bed. She held the back of the gown together as she rose. She didn't want to flash Max should he wake up.

"Cayla, should you be getting up?" Max said from the corner of the room.

"Yes, I can't bring the bathroom to me, so I have to get up, Maxwell. I'll be alright," she assured him.

He handed her a small suitcase. "I brought some things for you to put on."

Cayla looked at the small, expensive bag. "Thanks, Max," she said and went into the bathroom.

Max stretched his arms over his head. He needed that nap. He really felt refreshed.

A few minutes later, Cayla returned to the room and got back into the bed. "Max, you didn't get anything from my apartment. These things are all new."

Max didn't respond. He needed to talk to her seriously about her and her son's future. *Son.* He was calling her child a son when he really didn't know if it was a boy or girl, but Jon said *son* in the dream.

"How are you feeling today, Cayla?" he asked.

"Better, thank you."

"Good, because we have a lot to discuss," he said, pulling the chair closer to the bed.

"Like what?" Cayla asked apprehensively.

"Well, first I want to know what happened to you?" he asked and saw Cayla's body tense.

"Does it matter now, Max?" she said tersely.

"Hell yeah. You should have never been working in your condition. Jon would not have wanted this for you and his child."

"Well, Jon's not here, is he, Max? I did what I had to do to survive. You forget Jon did pick me up from the gutter - and I found my way back," she said angrily.

Max flinched. "Gutter?" Max said back to her, frowning.

"That's right, Max. How often have I heard that?" she said, defeated and angry. "Why did you buy new things for me? Didn't you go to my apartment?" she asked.

"Yes, as a matter of fact, I did," he answered, "and I want to know why you were living there, Cayla."

Cayla looked at him. Anger flowed through her veins, and something else - shame.

"Yes, Max, that is my home. It's not much, but it's clean."

"Clean, Cayla? I saw roaches climbing the walls," Max said incredulously.

"I did the best I could, Max, with what I had, so don't look down your aristocratic nose at me!"

"I'm sorry, Cayla. I'm not looking down on you. You just don't belong there."

"Belong there? That's where I came from or did you forget I wasn't born with a silver spoon in my mouth. I have to work for a living, especially now," she said harshly. "Just where do you think I belong, Max?"

"You can't stay there, Cayla. Where will you put the baby when he comes?"

"That is why I need to work. I've been saving for a bigger place," Cayla stated, her voice losing some of the harshness. She turned her head away, not wanting Max to see just how miserable and defeated she was. Max lifted her hand in his and squeezed it.

"Look at me, Cayla. Please."

Slowly her head turned.

"Do you think Jon would want this for you? He loved you from the moment he saw you, and I can't just sit by, knowing you are struggling to survive with his child inside you. Did you know how happy he was about the baby? I knew Jon all my life, and I had never seen him as happy as he was that day."

Cayla's eyes softened as she listened to Max. She remembered the day as if it were yesterday when she told him they were expecting their first child. They lay in the bed that night with his hand rubbing her then-flat stomach. He told her how wonderful their child's life would be, and then he kissed her stomach. Tears clouded in Cayla's eyes, and she pulled her hand from Max's.

"And do you think Jon would leave you without providing for you and your child's future?"

"No, Max. I know if Jon were here, this child would want for nothing.

However, Jon is not here, and he had just found out that I was pregnant. Maybe he didn't have a chance to make provisions for us. I understand that, and I'm not upset about that. I didn't love Jon for his money. I'd have loved the man even if he were dirt poor."

"Cayla, I know that, but Jon did provide for you and the baby. I know because I was a witness to it. The child will be my godchild."

Cayla gave him a sad smile. "Yes, Max, the child will be your godchild, but there was nothing, and it really doesn't matter. I will manage. If I'm nothing else, I am resilient."

"You don't understand, Cayla. Jon left you his entire estate and a handsome trust fund for the baby."

Cayla stared at him as if his head had just exploded.

"No, that's not what his mother..." Cayla stated then stopped.

"What, Cayla? What did his mother say?"

"Nothing - it doesn't matter. I don't want anything," she stated firmly.

"What do you mean you don't want it?" Max said, his voice rising. "This is your child's inheritance. You can't refuse it."

"I don't care. I will take care of my baby. I want nothing to do with the money or his family," she stated, her voice rising also.

"Cayla, Jon provided for his mother and sisters too; maybe not on the same scale as you and the baby, but he took care of them. What about the baby?"

"I will provide for my child," she said stubbornly. "Besides, they don't know about the baby. They may have taken..." she stopped speaking again. "Max, I don't want his estate," she said finally.

Max listened to her, understanding now. He even understood why she wanted nothing to do with Jon's mother. Mrs. Sherman did something, what - he didn't know, but he was not about to allow Cayla to refuse what is rightfully hers and

Jon's son. However, he wouldn't push her now about that.

"Cayla, I loved Jon too. I can't let you live as you are living now."

"What do you want from me, Max?"

"Let me help you."

Cayla turned from him. She didn't want his handouts or his pity.

"Please, Cayla, let me do this for my friend – please," Max implored. Cayla looked at him, searching his eyes.

"Okay, Max, I'll do this for my baby and just until I can do better," she conceded.

Max exhaled, smiling into her eyes. "You're a stubborn woman, Cayla Sherman," he said.

"So Jon used to say," she said and smiled.

"Everything's going to be okay now, I will see to that. I've found a small house that you can move in as soon as you're released. The only thing is that we have to furnish it. Are you up for decorating your home?"

Cayla smiled at Max. He was such a good man. She was surprised no one had snatched him up yet. She did know whomever he chose would be the luckiest woman in the world. She had no doubt Max would cherish the woman he fell in love with, just how Jon had cherished her.

"Yes, Max, I think I will be," she said, smiling. "Thanks, Max. I'll never forget this."

He smiled then leaned down and kissed her forehead. "Jon loved you, and you made him happy. It's the least I can do."

Chapter Three

Harriett Washington had invited Margaret over for lunch. "So, Margaret, have you heard anything from Jon's wife?" Harriett asked before she took a sip of her sweet tea.

"Please, why would I?" she said in that high-pitched superior tone.

Margaret Sherman was still a lovely woman with her graying hair. She was small in stature, with cold eyes and an equally cold heart. She had placed herself on a pedestal and thought everyone was supposed to look up to her. She tried that superior attitude on Harriett once; when she got done with Margaret, she stepped down from the elevated level on which she had placed herself, at least with her. Harriett knew Margaret before she had married so well. She may be able to fool her circle of wealthy friends, but she knew better than to come off superior to Harriett.

"So, you don't know how she is faring?" Harriett asked.

"Please, Harriett," Mrs. Sherman said with disgust. "She's gone. I got rid of her, and I put her out of this family's life permanently. I just wish Jon had talked to me before he married that gold-digger. I know I could have convinced him not to marry her."

"I thought they were a lovely couple, so much in love," Harriett commented.

"Lust was more like it. I loved my son, and I miss him terribly; but, he was such a bad judge of character." Harriett tensed.

"Where did she go?" Harriett asked.

"I have no idea, and I don't care. I will not allow that woman to get her hands on my son's estate."

Harriett had to bite her tongue to keep from saying anything; when what she wanted to do was curse the wench out.

"Jon did have a will, Margaret. Surely he left something for his wife?" Harriett stated.

"I found no will. Anyway, I am executrix of his estate, and it has always been that way."

"Surely that changed when he married Cayla."

"Regardless, I still hold his power of attorney."

"So, Cayla just *moved* from the home they shared?"

"Of course not, I had her evicted. I went over there and told her she had to leave. I even said she could have that horrible furniture she put in his condo. She just left everything." Margaret chuckled. "I even took the car Jon had bought for her. Actually, it only seemed fitting that since she came to Jon with nothing, she should leave with nothing, don't you think?" she asked, sipping her tea as if her attitude was the way to be.

Harriett stared at Jon's mother. Margaret Sherman is a real bitch, she thought.

"You do understand I had to protect Jon's estate; after all, she was not one of us," she said, trying to justify what she did to Cayla.

"One of us?" Harriett repeated. "Margaret, please. You forget I know where you came from, so don't put on airs for me," Harriett said truthfully.

Margaret stiffened, and her mouth dropped open. Harriett couldn't stand it one minute more. She rose from the chair.

"You know, Margaret, I knew you were heartless, but this is even worse for you. I want you to get up from that chair and get out of my house before I throw you out myself."

Margaret huffed, her mouth wide with shock. "Harriett, what is your problem?"

"You are my problem. You're a nasty, nasty little woman. That poor girl has no family. She only had Jon, and you evict her from her home?" Harriett paused, shaking her head. "You know what, Margaret? What goes around comes around. Heed my words. You will regret what you did to Jon's wife. Now get out of my house."

Margaret rose and left in a huff.

Harriett called Max and told him to meet her at her house when he left the hospital.

An hour later, Max was at his mother's house. She told him what Margaret had done and what she said to Margaret. Max laughed, telling his mother he knew she wouldn't be able to hold her temper.

After leaving his mother's house and while Cayla convalesced in the hospital, Max went to see Jack Borden. He was Jon's financial manager. Also meeting with them was their attorney, Mark Rodgers. He discovered Mrs. Sherman no longer held power of attorney nor was she the executor of Jon's estate. She was at one time, but Jon had nullified it when he and Cayla married. Cayla was sole executrix of his estate. Max wondered if Margaret Sherman knew that.

Mark said he tried to locate Cayla, but Mrs. Sherman told him she had left the state. Jack told Max if Mrs. Sherman hadn't known, she knew now because she tried to have Jon's estate transferred into her name, but her papers were invalid. So, Jon's estate is sitting there growing interest. Of course, Mrs. Sherman hired a lawyer to try and get it converted to her. "When I met with her lawyer, he said she didn't mention Jon having a wife," Jack replied.

"You did clarify that for him, didn't you?"

"Of course. When I spoke with Mrs. Sherman's attorney again, he said Mrs. Sherman would be contesting the will because Jon's wife deserved nothing, so I think Jon's wife will have a fight on her hands."

"No, she won't," Max said with confidence. "I know everything Jon wished. That's why I was his witness to all his legal documents. Also, this is strictly confidential, but Cayla carries Jon's son. Mrs. Sherman knows nothing about this, and I want to keep it that way."

Jack and Mark readily agreed.

Cayla was released, and as promised, Ms. Thompson had the house ready. She even had the landscape refreshed. Max smiled as he led Cayla up the cobblestone walk. Max hoped Cayla would like the house. He opened the door and let Cayla go ahead of him. He watched closely for her reaction. It meant a lot that she approved.

Cayla's eyes surveyed the rooms as she moved from one room to the other. She stopped in the master suite. Max was close on her heels.

She turned to Max, her face unreadable with mixed emotions.

"May I covert the sitting room in here to a nursery?" she asked Max.

"Anything you want, Cay. This is your home now."

"Max, this is temporary."

"Okay but still feel free to do whatever you want." Max watched her. Her small hand rested on her round belly. Dr. Bryant gave her the ultrasound, and they discovered that Cayla was carrying Jon's son. Max had been overjoyed in watching the little man resting inside his mother's womb. It was something to behold. How he wished his buddy could have experienced that moment. Man, what a feeling at that moment when the doctor said, "Ahh, look right there. See the little stem? Yes, we got ourselves a big ole boy." Max decided he would never take his dreams about Jon lightly again if he had any more of them.

"So, what do you think?" Max asked.

"I love it, Max. It's beautiful. Thank you."

Max smiled at her, and he was a little proud of himself.

"Now if you feel up to it, we can go shop for furniture. You're going to need a bed at least."

She agreed, and they were off again. Sitting in the car, Cayla looked over at

Max.

"Max, why haven't you ever married?" she asked out of the blue.

Max shrugged. "You mean the one that will give me heart palpitations? I don't know. I guess the right one hasn't come around yet."

"Do you ever want to get married? I do know how you and Jon loved women," she said laughingly.

Max smiled sheepishly. "Yes, we were known to be a little womanizing."

"A little? My goodness, the stories Jon told me made me believe you two were more than just a *little*. Why don't you try *Atomic Dogs,*" she replied, smiling at him as he blushed down to his toes.

"Well, you put a stop to that, didn't you?" he replied with a smile of his own.

"Jon knew the deal. He didn't want me to light him up," she stated arrogantly. Then Cayla got quiet, turned her head, and looked out of the window as tears threatened to fall.

Max glanced over at her. He reached out and touched her hand. Cayla looked over at him with tears glistening in her eyes.

"You alright?" he asked gently.

"I miss him so much, Max, you can't even imagine."

Max patted her hand. "I know, Cay. I do too, but it will get easier."

"Really? When Max? Tell me when, because I don't envision that happening during this lifetime. My heart breaks a little bit more every time I think of him and what our son will miss out on not knowing the wonderful man his father was. I still think of all the life lessons he would have instilled in him to make him a great man. I imagine all of the different footprints he would have helped him leave in this world. So again, tell me, Max. When will this get easier, and when will I stop thinking about everything that could have been?"

"You know, Cay, I can't give you a definite timeline on your feelings because he will forever be a part of you. And you don't want to forget everything anyway because you will use those things to help bring up your son to be the best he can be - as Jon would have. When my father died, man, I didn't think I was going to get over my grief. All I knew was I had to be strong for my mother. Then one day Jon came to me and told me how he felt when his father passed away. We talked about them until we were laughing and crying at the same time, just remembering them. So, think of the life you had together and the happy times you shared, plus, you haven't totally lost Jon. You carry a part of him inside you now that you can give all your love to."

Cayla's hand covered Max's. "You're right, Max, I do. Thank you for making me feel better."

He smiled and said, "Hey, it's my job."

Before the end of the day, Max and Cayla had purchased the furniture for the house and set up delivery for the same day. Cayla also discovered that Max was not a man who took *no* for an answer and was used to getting his way.

Cayla and Max now stood in her bedroom. Max had just finished helping her make the bed.

"Now, Cay, when I get back here tomorrow, this place better look as I left it. I don't want you doing anything until I get back."

"Max, didn't I say I wouldn't?"

"Yeah, but I distinctly remember Jon telling me he told you he would hire someone to paint the condo. But lo and behold, when he got home, you had the living room completely painted."

Cayla smiled. "He told you that, did he?"

Max nodded with his arms folded across his broad chest.

"Okay, I promise. Plus I'm too tired to even lift my arms. So, go on now and leave so I can go to bed."

"Good, I'll see you in the morning, okay?" Max said, turning to leave.

"Max, you don't have to do this. I could do this myself."

"I don't mind. I think, I like shopping with you," he said, surprising himself.

Cayla laughed. "Thanks, Max, but you do realize that we still have a lot of shopping to do, like for the kitchen, bathrooms, draperies, et cetera, et cetera?"

Max groaned and rolled his eyes upward. "Like I said, I think I like shopping with you. Goodnight, Cay. Sleep well."

Cayla and Max had the house completely furnished and partially decorated to Cayla's preference within two months of her moving in. Max hired who she needed to do all the heavy lifting and moving. Max noticed how much Cayla had blossomed. She worked with the builders well, telling them what to do and how she wanted things. She even drew them a sketch of her plans. She was a good designer. He knew Jon had made plans for her to open her own interior design business as soon as she got her degree. She really had an eye for color and fine lines. The workers respected her and went out of their way to please her.

Cayla had a unique personality. Everyone that met her liked her instantly except for Jon's family. They were truly missing out on a beautiful gem. He then discovered she was preparing lunch for the workers. Every day that they worked for her, she had a different meal prepared for them, not just some simple sandwiches. She was frying chicken, making pasta and stews, and creating desserts.

He came by one afternoon to find her serving the workers fried chicken and potato salad for lunch in the dining room. You would have thought there was a party going on with all of the loud laughter. He stood mesmerized, watching them interacting as if they had known each other for years.

"What am I paying you for?" he asked gruffly when the workers noticed him. Cayla got up from the table and stood in front of him with her hands on her hips, frowning up at him.

"Max, they are working. It's lunchtime; now you sit down and have some lunch," she said, pulling him to an empty chair.

He joined them and had to admit he did enjoy the lunch and the company. The crew was hilarious. They told Cayla to sit, and that they would clean up the kitchen. She fussed, but her fussing fell on deaf ears because the men cleaned everything spic and span before they returned to their duties. They had promised the house would be finished by day's end.

Max stopped by to see Cayla the next day. He found himself doing this almost every day. His excuse this time was that they still needed to shop for nursery furniture for his godson, which sounded lame to his own ears. She came to the door with a scarf tied around her hair and paint smeared on her cheek and nose. "What are you doing, miss?" Max asked, frowning at her.

"Hi, Max, come on in," she said, leaving him standing in the foyer. Max followed her to the back of the house. He found her sitting on a step ladder and painting cartoon characters on the wall of the nursery. She looked over at him. "Done!"

"It looks good, right?" she said, grinning at him. Max couldn't help but smile back. He went into the nursery and looked at the wall. It did look good.

"Yes, it does, Cay," he said, smiling.

"Hungry?" she asked as she looked up at him.

"Yes, but I thought I'd take you out to dinner tonight," he said. That was not the reason he stopped by, but that was the first thing that popped into his head when he saw her sitting there with paint on her face. Her tongue was in the corner of her mouth, and she was concentrating on her project and looking so sweet. His thought startled him.

"Really? Can we go to Varsity's? They have the best chili dogs and frosted orange drinks," she said excitedly.

"Varsity's?"

"Yeah, you ever been?"

"No."

"It's a drive-in restaurant - really laid back," she said, smiling.

"Okay, if that's what you want," he agreed.

"Let me change, and then we can be on our way."

They were now parked outside of Varsity's. Cayla was right; they did have good chili dogs. She ate two, and he was on his third one and drinking his second frosted orange drink.

"It's good, right?" she said, smiling at him.

"Exceptionally good," he said, laughing.

Max glanced over at Cayla. He found he looked forward each day to seeing her, and he thought about her all day, wondering what she was doing. He had to pull himself back. He was getting really attached to Cayla, and that was not healthy for either one of them. She was his best friend's wife, for God's sake. He couldn't – no, he *refused* to fall for her. He just liked her. She was a good friend. *Then why does your heart jump every time she smiles at you, fool? And in a minute, something else is gonna start jumping, so get a damn grip.*

"Max, are you dating?" she asked, pulling him from his thoughts.

He hadn't been on a date for several months, now that he thought about it. He had thrown himself into her welfare and the firm, forgetting all about himself.

"No, not lately."

"Why? Is it because of me? I seem to take up so much of your time."

"No, Cay. I've just been busy at the office, with Jon gone. I have a lot more to do."

"Oh. So find a partner to ease the load."

"No, this was Jon's and my dream. I'm fine with things the way they are."

"Okay, but I think maybe you should start dating again. You don't have to come by every night."

But I want to, his head said. "I know, Cay. Maybe I'll start again soon. Promise."

"Good. Are you finished or do you want another chili dog?" she said, laughing.

"I think I've had enough," he replied, smiling and patting his belly.

"Max, I want to ask you something. Now that I'm going into my eighth month, I was wondering if you would be my coach in the birthing classes. I promise not to take a lot of your time."

"Me?"

"Yes, why not? You're my son's godfather. Don't be scared," she laughed.

"What do I have to do?"

"Just coach me, give me support, and go into the delivery with me," she stated simply, hunching her shoulders.

Max's heart skipped a beat. He felt honored to do this for her and Jon. He was a little choked. He had to clear his throat a couple of times before he responded. "I would like that very much, Cay. Thank you."

"No; thank you, Max. You are such a good friend."

Yeah, but could there be more, Cayla? What the… he thought to himself. Max started to break out in a sweat. Aww Hell… He pulled in front of her house and walked her to the door. She looked up at him.

"We start next week at the hospital, okay?"

Max nodded and knew he needed to get out of there. He said his goodbye and hopped in his car, deep in thought. *Man. Oh. Man.*

Later that night, Max lay in his bed, thinking about Cayla. Across town, Cayla lay in her bed, thinking about Max. Both felt a storm coming.

Max was her rock in the midst of her storm. He came into her life and took care of her just like she knew Jon would have. So, what were these feelings she was having for Maxwell? She liked him; there was no doubt about that. He had been so good to her, and the more she saw of him, the more she wanted to see him. However, she knew she had to convince him to start seeing people because she was becoming too attached to Max, and that was not good. He was starting to become her world. She didn't want to think about what would happen when she moved out of his life and started a life of her own. She had to be strong enough to handle it for her sake and the baby. Still, after all of her self-talk, when she finally closed her eyes in slumber, it was Maxwell's face she saw, not Jonathan's.

Chapter Four

Cayla sat on the floor between Max's long legs with a pillow under her knees and her back leaning into his chest. Max's hands were on top of hers on her belly as they rubbed and breathed as the instructor told them. Cayla leaned back and looked up at him, smiling.

"You alright with this, Max?" she whispered.

Max looked down at her. How he wanted to kiss her beautiful mouth.

"Are you?" he countered.

She smiled up at him and turned her attention back to the instructor. Max looked down at her head. He was falling in love fast and hard with Cayla, and he couldn't stop it. He wasn't sure if he wanted to. *But she's your best friend's wife,* something in the back of his head said, *and you would do well to remember that.*

Cayla took his hand in hers and placed it on her stomach; Max's eyes widened in wonderment.

Wow. That was the first time he had ever felt the baby kick.

Cayla looked up at him, smiling. "Did you feel that?" she said

All Max could do was nod in astonishment. "Hey, there it goes again," he said in awe, smiling.

Cayla looked up at his smiling handsome face. Their eyes met, and they just gazed at each other.

"Mr. Washington," the instructor called, smiling. "Are you paying attention?"

Max's head shot up in embarrassment. "Yes, ma'am, I am," he said quickly. The moment was lost, to both Cayla's and Max's delight. Cayla thought for sure he was going to kiss her, and she would have probably kissed him back. He could feel Cayla's body shake with her laughter.

When Max dropped her off later that evening, he didn't stay. He wasn't sure he should, not with what almost happened in the class. He wanted badly to kiss her, and if the instructor hadn't interrupted him, he would have, that he would stake his life on.

Max and Cayla were at Babies R Us buying furniture for the nursery and clothes for the baby. Cayla asked, "Max, what do you think of this outfit?"

He was busy looking at the stuffed animals. He turned to her and was holding the ugliest gorilla she had ever seen. Cayla laughed. "That thing will give the baby nightmares," she laughed again. "Come here. I need your opinion," she said, holding up a blue and white outfit in front of her.

Max put the gorilla down and joined her. Max looked over the outfit. Cayla looked up at him, grinning.

"You trying to make my boy sweet?" Max said, frowning as he took the outfit and put it back on the rack.

"Oh, you would have him wearing a football uniform right from the womb," Cayla replied.

"Do they make them that small?" he asked, smiling impishly.

Cayla shook her head, moved away from him to the overly full cart, then moved to another rack.

Max was busy picking up an outfit he thought the baby would like, when he heard, "Maxwell, how are you?"

Max turned to see Sherri, Jon's youngest sister, and Mrs. Sherman coming toward him. Max looked down the aisle to see if he could see Cayla. He didn't want her to run into these two witches.

"Hello, Mrs. Sherman, Sherri," he said blandly.

"Maxwell, whatever are you doing in a baby store?" Sherri asked, looking at the outfits in his hand.

Just then, Cayla came around the corner, pushing the cart. Max closed his eyes briefly. Cayla stopped in her tracks when she saw her former mother-in-law. Her heart began to pound in her chest.

"Is that Cayla?" Mrs. Sherman asked, surprised yet impertinent. She went over to her.

"Max, I know you're not with Cayla?" Sherri asked, glaring at him.

"Yes, Sherri, as a matter of fact, I am," Max said coolly.

"So, Cayla, what brings you from the ghetto?" Mrs. Sherman asked nastily.

"Look, Mrs. Sherman, I have nothing to say to you, so if you will excuse me..."

"No, I will not. If you think you are going to get Jon's estate, you have another think coming!"

Cayla frowned. "What are you talking about?" Cayla stared at her. She had no idea what that woman was talking about. Cayla moved from the back of the cart to get away from that woman. Mrs. Sherman's mouth dropped open.

"Pregnant! You're pregnant, and Jon hasn't been in the ground a year? You bitch. I knew you were nothing but a whore!" she screamed at Cayla.

Cayla said nothing, just moved away from her. Mrs. Sherman grabbed her arm.

"Don't you walk away from me when I'm talking to you!"

Cayla looked down at her hand on her upper arm.

"Get your hands off me," Cayla said with warning in her tone.

"Don't you take that tone with me," Mrs. Sherman yelled in her face.

Cayla snatched her arm from her grasp.

Max was over to Cayla in an instant and stood in front of Mrs. Sherman.

"If you ever put your hands on her again, I will personally have you brought up on charges!" he spoke with hardness in his tone.

"Maxwell, don't tell me you have been duped by this bitch too, just like my son!"

"If I were you, Mrs. Sherman, I would refrain from calling her names," Max suggested to her coolly. Cayla placed her hand on Max's arm.

"It's okay, Max," Cayla said softly.

"No, it's not, Cayla," Max responded.

"Maxwell, you were Jon's best friend. I cannot believe that you're with her. She's pregnant by another man, and Jon's not gone a year yet. Didn't waste any time, did you, you little strumpet!" Sherri yelled at her.

"That's enough!" Max bellowed. "Cayla is no longer your concern, so I suggest you and your daughter go on your way - now!"

Sherri and Mrs. Sherman's mouths dropped opened.

"Max, I can't believe you let her sucker you in like she did Jon," Sherri commented snidely.

"What I am doing with Cayla is of no concern of yours. I think you should be more worried about the karma that will surely come back on you for your poor treatment of Jon's wife," he said before he and Cayla walked away.

During the weeks that followed, Cayla grew heavier with child and was anxious to give birth. Max doted on her unmercifully despite her resistance.

Mrs. Sherman called Max's mother to tell her how he had treated her and Sherri. Harriett Washington simply said, "Then you should have minded your own business."

Weeks later, in the middle of the night, Cayla was awakened by pains in her lower abdomen. She rose from the bed clumsily. Her water broke and gushed down her legs. Cayla calmly called her doctor then made her way to the bathroom and got into the shower. After dressing, she sat for a while and monitored her contractions, per her doctor's instructions. Cayla talked to her baby, telling him that she couldn't wait to meet him. She was nervous *and* excited. When the pains became closer, she called Max.

"Max, it's Cayla. The pains have started. They're ten minutes apart."

"Cayla, why didn't you call me sooner? I'll be right there!" he said anxiously, stumbling and hitting his toe on the chair.

Cayla went to the living room and waited for Max. He arrived in less than five minutes.

"Did you call the doctor?" he inquired in a voice was on the verge of panic as he rushed through the door.

"Yes, I called him earlier. He said when the contractions got to ten minutes apart, I should come on in. He's there already."

"Cay, why didn't you call me?"

"I did call you," Cayla said, smiling.

"Cayla, this is not a laughing matter."

"Max, I think you need to drive me to the hospital."

"Yeah--yeah, you ready?"

Cayla nodded. With her bag in his hand, Max took Cayla's arm and they left.

They were greeted in the maternity ward by a young nurse. Now prepped, Cayla lay on the bed. She was having contractions, and the nurse inquired if she attended the birthing classes. When she nodded, the nurse turned to Maxwell and said, "Your job will be to remind her to relax and breathe properly." Maxwell took Cayla's hand in his, reminding her to breath quick and shallow. He timed the length of the contractions and the minutes in between.

As the nurse moved to raise the bed to an inclined position, Cayla lay back. Max stood on the other side of the bed, still holding her hand. Once settled, she looked up at him; his attention was on the nurse giving further instructions about his duties. Absently Max caressed Cayla's hand as he listened intently. He looked down at her and their eyes met. Max smiled.

Dr. Bryant entered the room and greeted them. "Okay," the kind-hearted doctor said, "Cayla, let's see how far along you are," he said, going to the foot of the bed and lifting the sheet over her knees. "Try to relax and tell me if a contraction should start while I'm checking you." Max stood beside her, her hand in his.

"Should I leave?" he asked the nurse.

"No, Max, don't go - please," Cayla said with a tremble in her tone. Her hand gripped his harder. She was getting more nervous.

Max smiled down at her and squeezed her hand.

When the doctor finished his examination, he pulled down her gown and pulled the covers over her legs. He moved to the side of the bed and lightly stroked the wide base of Cayla's abdomen.

"Here comes one, Cayla. Now just relax with it and count. Cayla's hand gripped Max's like a vise. Beads of sweat broke out on her forehead, her eyes closed tightly, and her mouth became tight.

"Open your mouth, Cay," he reminded her softly. "Pant in little breaths."

Even through her pain, she was happy. Max was there, and the baritone timbre of his voice soothed her. Her eyes opened and a tear slid down the side of her face, disappearing into her hair.

After the contraction dissipated, Cayla spoke. "Max, I'm so happy you're here,"

Max smiled at her. "Me too, Cay."

"Cayla, here... give me your hand." The doctor took Cayla's hand and placed it low around her stomach, "Mr. Washington, put your hand here on the other side. Now wait, you will feel it when it starts. The muscles will tighten, starting at the sides, and the stomach will arch and change shape during the contraction. When it ends, the muscles will relax and settle down." Just then, Max and Cayla's fingertips touched as they cradled the base of her stomach. Together they shared the discovery and exhilaration as the contours of her abdomen changed. Max stared in total amazement at what was happening beneath his hand. The joy that filled his heart at just the touch of the life she carried inside, his best friend's son moving under his hand, brought tears to his eyes. Instantly Max knew he would love this child with all his heart and soul.

Cayla threw her arms over her head and gripped the headboard of the bed. Max pulled his eyes away from Cayla's stomach to face her and found her holding the headboard in a viselike grip. Her lips were pursed, and her jaws were clenched against the pain. Max leaned over her, smoothing her hair from her sweating forehead. Her mouth relaxed and fell open. He spoke softly, reminding her in quiet tones to breathe and relax. When the pain receded, Cayla took his hand in hers.

"Max, I'm scared," she whispered hoarsely.

Cayla looked over at her doctor. "It's natural to be afraid; this is your first baby. But trust me, you will lose that fear once this little one is ready to make an appearance," the doctor told her with a smile. "As the pains get closer, it will be more important to relax, and that, Mr. Washington, is your job - to keep her relaxed. It will help if you rub the tummy lightly, like this. I like to think the baby can feel it too."

Max sat on the side of the bed, his hand replaced the doctor's, and he gently rubbed Cayla's stomach. Cayla looked at Max and gave him a small shaky smile before her eyes closed.

"Good, I think you can take over, Mr. Washington. I'll be back in a few minutes," he said softly and left the room.

Cayla's eyes were closed, her right arm thrown over her forehead. She was relaxed and breathing naturally. A satisfied light came into his eyes. He knew then this was where he was supposed to be, right here beside her. Her flawless nutmeg face, now full and healthy, was a striking comparison to her face the night he found her walking up the street. *Beautiful* was all he could think of when he looked at her: her perfect oval face, her temptingly curved mouth, and exquisitely dainty nose. Her lush lashes swept down across her cheekbones. Yes, *beautiful* was all he could think of to describe her.

Cayla's eyes opened, and what she saw in his eyes made her gasp. His eyes brimmed with a tenderness that she felt without words.

"Max," Cayla called his name softly, reaching her hand toward him. His large hand took hers and held it as his other caressed her stomach. He smiled.

"You're doing so well, Cay. It won't be long before this little one will be in your arms."

"Thank you, Max, for everything, I don't…" She couldn't finish as a pain suddenly gripped her. She pulled her hand from his and gripped the headboard.

"Relax and breathe, Cay," Max instructed as he rubbed her and breathed with her. "Look at me, Cay." Her eyes opened.

"That's it, baby. It's almost over."

"Oh, Max, I don't think I can do this," she said, panting.

"Yes, you can. I'll be right here the whole time."

Cayla gave him a weak smile and closed her eyes.

When they came to wheel her to the delivery room, Max was still beside her, dressed in hospital scrubs, holding her hand and saying encouraging words. In the delivery room, Max stood above her head and continued to talk soothingly and encouragingly. After the fifth contraction, Jonathan Thomas Sherman II was born. Tears of joy coursed down Max's and Cayla's face when he cut the cord and the baby was placed on her chest. Max leaned over and kissed Cayla so tenderly on her lips that tears again filled her eyes. He then looked at the child. Max was taken aback at how much the baby boy looked like Jon. Everything on that small face was Jon; he could see nothing of Cayla. He had gotten his best friend back. Max turned his gaze from the child and looked at Cay. She was asleep. He smiled and again kissed her gently on her mouth.

Dr. Bryant looked at them, smiled and thought, *Yep, looks like those two need each other, and they look good together.*

Already three months had passed, and Max was there every day. Sometimes after the baby was down for the night, Cayla and Max would talk until way past the midnight hour. It amazed her how she had opened up to him about Jon and her past life. Cayla also knew Max loved Little Jonathan with all his heart.

"It amazes me," Max said, stunned as they stood over the baby's crib. "No offense, Cay, but he looks nothing like you. It's like God has given us back Jon."

Cayla put her hand in his. Max looked down at her and smiled. She looked up at him.

"He's beautiful," was all she could say.

"Come, Cay. We really need to talk."

They left the room. It was time to let Cayla know that Mrs. Sherman was contesting Jon's will. In order for them to fight, he needed Cay.

Cayla sat on the sofa and pulled her bare feet under her butt. Max sat across from her in one of the high back chairs. His face was unreadable and serious.

Cay frowned. "Max, what's wrong?"

Max took a breath. "Mrs. Sherman is contesting Jon's will and the estate," he told her.

Max watched as she visibly tensed. The Sherman family was a sore subject with them. Cayla never wanted to talk about them.

"So?" Cayla responded. "I told you I didn't want the estate, Maxwell."

"Cayla, this is your son's legacy. Everything Jon owned he left to you and the…"

Cayla came to her feet suddenly.

"No, Max. I don't want those people in my life or my son's life. I will not allow them to make my son feel like he is inferior to them. No, Max, I don't want it," she said, glaring at him with burning, reproachful eyes.

Max came to his feet. "Why should you care what those ignorant people think, Cay? They don't have to be in your life."

Cayla turned from him, her arms folded around her body.

"Cayla," Max called her name softly. "You knew the magnitude of Jon's love for you and the baby. Do you honestly think he would be pleased to know that everything he worked hard for would not go to ensure the comfort of his wife and child? He would be crushed."

Cayla remained quiet. Max dropped his head, almost in defeat.

"So now what, Cay? Do I just let Mrs. Sherman take all that Jon left for his family? I will not see you working three jobs to make ends meet, Cay. What about his son? Do you want him growing up in a project somewhere when he doesn't have to? Is that what you want? Swallow that stubborn pride, Cay, and think about someone else for once," Max said none too gentle to her. It was time for truth.

Cayla turned to him. Tears wavered in her eyes as she looked at him.

"You don't understand, Maxwell. When she finds out about my son and sees him, she will try to take him from me. She has the means, and she's been demeaning me ever since Jon and I married."

Max went to her, pulling her arms from around her body. Cayla looked up at him.

"And so do you. First, you will claim your son's and your inheritance, then you can fight her with everything you have. However, I don't think she would dare try to take Jon's son from you. She has nothing to stand on."

"Don't think she won't try when she realizes that Jonathan is her grandson. Right now she thinks he's someone else's, and I want her to continue to think just that," Cayla stated with finality.

Max smiled. "So, you will claim your inheritance?"

"Yes, Max, for my son, I will."

"Good, now let's sit and discuss what it entails. You don't really know how wealthy you are."

When Max finished telling Cayla about the particulars of the estate, she was stunned into silence. "Max, what am I going to do with all of that? I have never had so much in my life."

"Just leave everything with your financial manager. Jon had been with him for years, and he's an honest man. He'll take care of your money and investments," Max assured her.

"What about the cars, Max? I don't need all those cars."

"Sell them if you want. You can do whatever you want with them."

Cayla dropped her head, trying to digest all that Max had told her. She was rich. She lifted her head.

"Thank you, Max," she spoke softly. "I'm still not sure I want all this for myself, but I will proceed for my son." She shook her head.

It was enough for him. Max smiled and rose from the chair. He pulled her up from the sofa and into his arms. Cayla stiffened at first then she relaxed and laid her head on his chest, her arm circling his waist. Max's hand caressed her back tenderly.

"It's my job," he said simply.

Cayla raised her head and looked up at him. A subtle, sensuous light passed between them. She saw the heart-warming tenderness in his gaze, and her heart turned over in response, jolting and elevating her pulse.

His large hands cradled her face gently. Cayla knew she should pull away, but her body would not obey. Her eyes closed as she savored his touch. Her tongue darted out and licked her now dry lips.

"I'm going to kiss you, Cayla," he stated seductively.

"I know," she said before her eyes opened. When his head lowered to her, her eyes closed again. She felt his lips touch hers like a whisper. The touch of his lips on hers sent a shock wave through her entire body. Her mouth opened with no coaxing from him. She felt his warm tongue as it swept into her mouth, and she purred, returning his ardor. Her arms inched up around his neck, holding him to her as his demanding mouth caressed hers. She'd never experienced anything so soul-stirring since Jon, and she didn't want him to stop. His head lifted. His dark eyes were hooded as he gazed at her face. She put her hands on his warm face and gazed silently into his eyes. She felt heat radiating through her body. She was on fire. She wanted him to hold her; she wanted to touch him all over as well. She longed for someone to love her again. Frantically, she pulled the shirt from his pants then worked at the buttons. Max froze, although his powerful chest moved in deep, labored breaths.

"Cayla..." His voice was low and strained. "Do you know what you're doing?"

Recklessly, she pushed the shirt open, baring him to her. He was a magnificent creature, his body a tightly knit masterpiece of strength and muscularity. Cayla touched him lightly, spreading her hands on his sculptured chest as the toned muscles flexed beneath her hands. She licked his nipples while stroking the hard-rippled surface of his stomach. Her fingers followed the light dusting of hair that disappeared into the waistband of his pants then cupped him and squeezed. "Does it feel like I know what I'm doing, Max?"

He made a sound deep in his throat. Max caught her wrists, holding her arms away from him. He stared at her hard. "Yes, you definitely know what you're doing, but if you touch me again, I'm not sure I'll be able to stop. Do you understand? So, be sure you're ready for me, baby."

Cayla licked him again while looking into his hooded eyes. She knew she should stop but she couldn't; she needed this. She needed him. So, she licked him again and again until he grasped her head and urgently kissed her until she didn't know if she was coming or going.

She stepped back and removed her shirt then unhooked the front closure of her bra, letting it float to the floor. Max pulled Cayla back into his arms, and his mouth devoured hers. When he grabbed her tongue and tugged, she had to hold onto him for fear of hitting the floor. She felt his hands on her bottom, pushing her into the hardness of his massive manhood. If he felt this good with his pants on, she was in for a wild ride. "Umm," Cayla moaned when his warm mouth trailed light kisses down her neck. Then he backpedaled and bit her ear before circling his tongue inside and blowing. Cayla hunched her shoulders, panting his name. She tried to move away, but he wouldn't let her. He left her ear and took her heavy breast in his mouth. He licked, popped, squeezed, and bit one then the other.

He felt her flinch. He raised his head, gazing at her. "Did I hurt you?" he asked huskily. "You taste so damn good, girl, I got carried away."

She shook her head. Again, he lowered his head and kissed her between her breasts, all the while squeezing and massaging as if he couldn't get enough. Quiet, incoherent sounds filtered from her throat. All she knew was that Max had a sleek, muscled body and an amorous, sexy mouth, and she was going to savor and enjoy every moment he gave. All her being was focused on the man who held her so intimately against his hard body.

Suddenly he lifted her and sat with her on the sofa, her legs straddling his hips while his mouth played havoc on her neck. She felt his hands lightly moving up her skirt, caressing and tantalizing the skin in his path. His featherlight fingertips found the junction between her legs and played a game of rub and pull. Her body melted and she could feel the wetness there. Dang, he had her soaked with just a touch, and he wasn't even inside of his sweetness yet. Her head fell on his strong shoulder. She gasped when his fingers finally slipped inside of her. It seemed like something combusted in her, and she rode his fingers. *Ahh, what a feeling.* She kissed, sucked and traced her tongue along the cords in his neck, biting him. She was getting more turned on by the second. Suddenly, he drew his hand away from her wetness. She felt the hard heaviness of his manhood being released from his pants. He moved a little and wedged himself between her legs, touching her damp opening. Cayla trembled as she felt him ease inside her, stretching her delicate flesh. She sucked air through her teeth. "Ah, that's it, Max," she moaned before she said nasty little things in his ear. She'd bet he didn't know that he would release her alter ego…Ms. Dirty….

"Am I hurting you? Should I take it slow?" he asked as his gaze raked over her face.

Cayla breathed out, "No. I love things dirty, hard, and fast." Needing no more encouragement, he went to work. He slipped his hand between them, and he adjusted her to take all of him. Abandoning herself completely, she took all he had to offer and began the dance of a woman without any inhibitions.

She was riding him so hard that Max had to close his eyes and bite his lips to keep from crying out like a little punk. She took his head in her small hands, claiming his mouth hungrily. She sucked the juice out of his lips before going in for the kill. She twirled her tongue around his, capturing it in a cat and mouse game. She thought that the next time she would see how long it took to get to the center of his *tootsie pop* when she showed him what her dirty little mouth could really do. But for now, she would ride him into the sunset. Max was having thoughts of his own. His hands were on her hips, urging her against him in an insistent rhythm as he thrust deep and hard. He thought if he went any further he would be in her lungs. Woweee. He kept kissing her until Cayla pulled away, gasping. A strange wild fever had taken over, and she couldn't stop herself from moving against him. The only sound in the room was the sound of pleasure that came from both of them while their bodies slapped hard. She loved the thrusting of his body inside her, and she loved the scent of him. Her mouth rained kisses on his face as she rode him harder and harder. Then suddenly she couldn't move. Her muscles seemed to lock as a burning pleasure blossomed in her loins and spread through her body. She'd never felt anything like it. She felt Max's arms tighten around her as his hips still thrust upward in her. She raised her head, surprised at how he was making her feel. She moaned, and her body tightened in wonderful spasms around his manhood. That was enough to send him over the edge as well. His hands gripped her bottom and pulled her against him while he moved deeper inside her. She felt it when he got harder and exploded. *Damn, now that's what I'm talkin' 'bout...*

Feeling lightheaded, Cayla rested her head on his shoulder. Max was rubbing her bare back soothingly. She remained in that position for a few minutes. Then the reality of what had just happened hit her. She raised her head and looked at Max. His head lay back, eyes closed.

"What did we do?" she asked softly. Max opened his eyes.

"What?"

"What have I done?" she repeated woefully, lifting herself from him. She looked frantically for her shirt. The guilt of her actions bombarded her mind.

"Max, I'm so sorry I did..." she never finished. She ran from the room.

Max stood, stunned and now understanding.

"My God," he whispered. He'd just made love to his best friend's wife. What happened to the control he prided himself on? Then the guilt of what happened hit him square in his gut painfully.

"I'm sorry, Jon," he whispered before getting dressed and leaving the house. Max sat outside her house, looking up at it. Why did he do that, he asked himself? It was too soon for this. He loved her, and the guilt of loving his friend's wife overwhelmed him. Is he so starved for love that he takes his friend's wife? *But you're in love with her, you fool,* he chided himself. *So why did you run?* Damn it, what now? Why didn't she push him away? Did she feel the same way? No, she needs time to grieve, Max told himself. It was time to put space between them. He remembered her suggesting he should date, and that is what he was going to do. After the estate was settled, he would ease out of her life, find someone of his own, and wean away from this absurd infatuation he had with Cayla and her son. But man, what a connection. They could be so good together. Shit, what am I to do? What am I to do? I just jacked things up. *Maann...*

Later that night, Max was dreaming of his friend.

Tears rolled down his face as he talked to his friend. "You've seen him?"

"Of course... he looks just like me. Tell him about me, Max. Tell him I love him very much, and I will be watching over him. Max, just remember there is only love. Fill your life with it while you can. I know it won't be easy. There are obstacles you and Cay will have to get over, but if you love her as I feel you do, it will be easy. Love her, Max, with all your heart." Then he was gone.

Max awoke with a start and sat up in the bed. "Jon," he whispered and then cried until no more tears came. He still felt he needed to give Cayla space. It was wrong for him to be in love with his best friend's wife. *But she makes me feel complete. Jon, help me, man....I don't know what to do. I feel so guilty. Help me, bruh...Please."*

****

It had been a full three weeks since that night, and Max was still having difficulty forgetting how she felt in his arms, and he missed his son... Jonathan's son, he corrected himself. He chastised himself severely, but he could not forget Cayla. In the meantime, he had met the beautiful Bianca Steele while he was having dinner alone. Actually, she approached him, and he thought why not? Bianca was tall, athletically built and very health conscience due to her aversion to fat people - her words. She was Afro-Latin American and a flawless beauty with pecan complexion, brown doe-shaped eyes, and full mouth - quite the opposite of Cayla.

Bianca was an executive VP for a thriving forty-four-year-old organization headquartered in Cincinnati, Ohio. They were a global operation and had recently opened a branch in Atlanta. She had worked her way from the bottom to the top, which she talked about often. She was a bit controlling and self-centered, but then he guessed she had to be to get to where she was. She had called all the shots in the few weeks that they had dated. She decided where they would go, what they would do, and even what they would order off the menus. She even initiated intimacy, but that was also done to her specification. If he initiated affection, he was quickly shut down. Her personality was questionable, but she was a means to an end: it kept him from thinking about Cayla - sometimes.

Max glanced down at his watch and cursed. He was late. He should have been at Bianca's condo thirty minutes ago. He would never hear the end of his tardiness. He pressed the button with her number that she assigned on his phone; of course, it was the number one. They were going to his mother's house for dinner. He felt it was too soon for that, but Bianca, he learned quickly, was like a dog with a bone when it came to something she wanted - and she wanted to meet Harriett Washington. So, to end the debate of why he didn't want her to meet his mother, he conceded. Of course, he told his mother that he was bringing Bianca for dinner, and his mother gave him that understanding motherly smile and replied that she looked forward to meeting her.

Bianca picked up on the first ring. "Maxwell, where are you?" she snapped.

"Late meeting; I'm leaving now," he lied.

"Fine, but we have to work on your punctuality. I don't like to be kept waiting. I thought you knew that about me by now," Bianca lectured.

Max rolled his eyes. "I'm on my way," he said before disconnecting.

As he drove to Bianca's condo, he kept asking himself why he was even with her. Oh yeah, Cayla, his best friend's wife, he reminded himself. But soon, he would have to let Bianca know that she was not dealing with a punk. He was only letting her have her way and calling the shots until he got his head screwed back on straight.

When he parked beside her BMW, he could see her standing in the window looking out at him. Max took a deep breath and got out of the car. He waited to see if she would at least open the door for him since he knew that she saw him. No, not Bianca; she waited until he rang the doorbell four times before she answered the door. It took everything in him not to tell her to get over herself and then leave her there, but he didn't.

When she did answer, she simply said, "How does it feel to be kept waiting?" She closed the door and walked past him.

Max couldn't believe this shit. Flabbergasted, he stared at her as she stopped beside the passenger door with her hands clasped demurely in front of her, waiting. He took another deep breath and thought again about why he was putting himself through this hell that is named Bianca. He was honest with himself but shook his head. He was punishing himself for making love with his best friend's wife. He went to the car, opened the door and closed it once Bianca got settled.

The whole trip Bianca didn't say a word. He could foresee this night becoming a huge disaster if Bianca kept up with her attitude; because his mother was not the one. His mother would step to her without a second thought.

A few minutes later, they were pulling into his mother's driveway. He turned his head and looked over at the fuming Bianca. Her eyes scanned the exterior of the house he was raised in. It was one of those large white two-story antebellum homes with its tall colonnades extended around the house, a portico covering the balcony on the second floor, and tall windows in the front.

She looked over at him. "Well, Maxwell, let's go meet your mother," she said as if it was an imposition to her.

Max shook his head and got out of the car to open her door. At the front door, while they waited for his mother to answer, Bianca looked over at him and rolled her eyes impatiently.

"Is your mother feeble and can't answer the door? Maybe you need to consider getting her a maid for such things," she commented.

"Bianca, hold the attitude because I am not for your mess. She was probably in the kitchen," he answered.

"Don't you at least have a key?" she snapped.

"Yes, but this is my mother's home, and we will wait, or I can take your behind right back home!" Max replied harshly.

Bianca's eyes widened, for Max had never spoken harshly to her. He was usually like a little lap dog. However, before she could respond to his rudeness, the door opened. The transformation in Bianca was quick as lightning. The smile that spread on her face made you think just seconds ago they were a happy, loving couple.

Harriett stepped aside to let them enter. Max kissed his mother, took Bianca's coat, and hung it on the coat tree before making introductions.

"Mom, this is Bianca Steele; Bianca, my mother, Harriett Washington," Max introduced.

Harriett opened her mouth to speak but was interrupted.

"Harriett, it is nice to finally meet you. I've been after Maxwell to introduce us, but you know men. If you don't stay on them… well, I'm sure you understand."

Harriett's eyes shifted to her son, eyebrows raised. *Oh no this little heifer didn't just go there with me. Um hum,* she thought. "It's nice to meet you as well," Harriett said, extending her hand. She was left hanging, however, when Bianca moved out of the foyer and into the parlor. Harriett fumed. *One more nasty little thing and you are going to be out on your little butt, missy,* she thought

"What an interesting home you have, Harriett," she called from the other room.

"Where in the hell did you find her? Where ever you found her, you need to take her back," Harriett whispered and frowned before following the aggressive dinner guest.

Max just shook his head and followed his mother. He found Bianca looking at some of the antiques his mother had sitting around the parlor that had been in their family for generations.

Bianca turned and gave them a tight smile, although disapproval shone in her eyes. "You really seem to like old things, Harriett," she commented.

"Yes, this room has a lot of history, and I like to display my heritage. All these things were passed down from generation to generation and will one day belong to Max, along with the house which has been designated as a historical home. Did you know…"

"How quaint," she interjected, interrupting Harriett. "If Max and I marry one day, we will have to discuss that," she said with that same tight smile on her face.

Harriett tensed and was ready to throw this uppity little wench out of her house, but she quelled the urge for Max's sake. "Dinner will be ready in a minute. Shall we sit and get acquainted?" Harriett invited.

Bianca sat on the antique French sofa and patted the seat beside her for Max to sit, like some lap dog.

Max ignored her and remained standing. "Mother," he said, waving his hand for her to sit.

"Can I get you something to drink, Ms. Steele?" Harriett asked before she sat.

"No, thank you. If I want something, I'm sure Maxwell wouldn't mind getting it," she said haughtily.

This little girl is going to mess around and get her feelings hurt up in here, Harriett thought.

Harriett took a seat across from her. "Well, Ms. Steele, Max tells me you are new to Atlanta. How are you enjoying our fair city so far?"

"It's a little overpopulated for my taste, but I'll adjust. I'm the VP for my company, and they needed me to come down and oversee the new branch they opened. So being a team player, I made the move anyway."

"Well, you could always move to a more suburban town," Harriett offered with a tight smile of her own.

"Yes, that could be an option in the future, I guess," she commented. She looked over at Max. "I'd like that drink now, so be a dear and get me a glass of red wine, Max," she said, then looked at Harriett. "You do have red wine?"

Max rose. "Would you like a glass, Mother?"

Harriett rose, already sick of this wench. "We might as well have dinner then," she said, leaving the room.

Bianca stood beside Max. "Remind me to give your mother the name of my decorator," she said as if it were her right.

"Maybe you should tell her at dinner. I'm sure she will appreciate any advice you have," Max replied mischievously.

Max led her to the nicely set table and helped his mother first with her chair. Bianca cleared her throat to get Max's attention. Ignoring her, he sat his mother.

"Maxwell, should you have not helped me with my seat first?" she asked tightly.

Max looked over at her and almost told her to sit her ass down, but he refrained. When he moved to help her, she pulled the chair out and sat without his assistance. Max shrugged and went to the seat at the head of the table. Harriett tucked her lips in to hide her smile.

After grace was said, Max and Harriett started to serve themselves while talking about Harriett's day and the latest fundraising committee she was leading. Neither initially noticed that Bianca had not moved to serve herself. They both stopped what they were doing and looked at her.

"Bianca, is there something wrong?" Max asked. His mother had prepared a nice meal of roast beef and potatoes, collard greens and homemade rolls, and everything looked delicious.

"I thought you would serve me, Maxwell," she replied sternly.

Harriett rolled her eyes. Her son was not going to wait on this heffa if she had anything to say about it, and she did.

"Ms. Steele, we are very informal here. Please help yourself," Harriett replied tightly.

Bianca glared across the table at Max, but she began to serve herself as Harriett and Max's conversation resumed.

"Harriett, you have my permission to call me Bianca," she said as she served herself small portions of the dinner and began to eat. That was it for Harriett. Who did this wench think she was? *Give me permission*, my ass.

Max looked over at his mother and knew she was fed up. She pushed her chair from the table, just as Bianca was putting a forkful of food into her mouth. Harriett reached over and snatched the fork out of her hand, surprising Bianca, who looked confused.

"Maxwell, it is time for your dinner guest to leave," she calmly announced. Max tried to hide the smile that threatened to come.

"I beg your pardon?" Bianca replied, still completely and ignorantly confused.

"I said it's time for you to go. You walked into my home as if it was supposed to be an honor for us to have you grace us with your presence. You've made nasty comments about my home, and I'm supposed to be *alright* with your rudeness? But what really pissed me off is, after coming in here and right away calling me by my given name, you give me *permission* to address you by your given name - like I was beneath you or just plain old stupid! You are the most disrespectful woman I've ever met!"

Harriett's voice rose. "I want you out of my house, and if Max had any sense, he would kick your narrow behind to the curb."

Harriett looked at Max. "Get that woman out of my house before I put her out myself," Harriett hissed. She left the room before she snatched Bianca's hair out from the roots.

Bianca remained in her seat, stunned. "What did I do?" she asked, confused and looking at Maxwell.

"You really don't understand, do you?" Max said, shaking his head. "Never mind, let's go, Bianca."

"Had I known I was going to be treated so rudely, Maxwell, I would not have accepted your invitation," she snapped, rising from the chair.

"Accepted?" Max repeated incredulously. "You pushed me into your meeting my mother. You better be glad I'm a gentleman, or your behind would be in a cab. So let's go before my mother returns, and trust me, you don't want that," he said, walking out of the dining room with Bianca following close behind.

The ride back to her place was tense. Several times Bianca looked at him as if to say something, but she remained quiet until he was pulling into the parking space beside her car.

Max unhooked his seatbelt to get out of the car.

"I can't believe you allowed your mother to treat me like that?" she pouted.

This girl is certifiably crazy. Max looked at her as if she had lost her mind. "You walk into my mother's home with that superior attitude, with your nose in the air, and being insulting. You disrespect my mother by not addressing her as Mrs. Washington. Then you give her *permission* to use your first name. Unbelievable. And, you expect me to defend you when you were wrong, Bianca. Furthermore, we have only been dating exclusively for three weeks, yet you have tried to control and rule me - but that's my fault. So, this will be goodbye. I hope you find what you are looking for because it sure as hell isn't me."

She opened the door to the car. "I will give you time to think about what happened tonight, and when you are ready to apologize, I'll be waiting for your call. Goodnight, Maxwell. Don't keep me waiting too long." She got out of the car as if he had not just told her seconds ago it was over.

Max shook his head and backed out of the parking space. "Yep... certifiably crazy." He was glad that was over. "I dodged a bullet on that one."

The next day, Max sat in the kitchen with his mother, having breakfast. He was very quiet. Harriett watched her son closely. She knew something was bothering him.

"What's wrong, Son?"

Max looked up at his mother. "Mom, I think I'm in love with Cayla," he stated.

"Really? Then why did you bring that crazy woman to my house?"

"Bianca was a distraction. I was just dating her to get over Cayla and my guilt, but it's not working." Max lowered his head. "I can't stop thinking about her and the baby."

"And this is a problem?"

"Yeah, well, Mom, she's Jon's wife. I can't fall in love with her."

"Why not? You are both single. If it were not for you, Son, where do you think Cayla and the baby would be? And if you don't realize it, Cayla is no longer Jonathan's wife."

"I know that too, but it just doesn't seem right that I fell in love with my best friend's wife," he groaned.

"Maybe she feels the same way as you do."

"I doubt it. She once told me she will never love again like she loved Jon."

"Well, of course not. You're not Jon. She will love you for who you are if she loves you."

Harriett smiled. "I've never seen you so unsure of yourself, Max," she commented.

"I know, Mom. I am unsure of myself. I don't know what to do. It's not right for me to be in love with her. I feel like I'm stabbing my best friend in the back. She's Jon's wife," he huffed. "I tried not seeing her, but then I found myself going to her house anyway. She's even encouraging me to date. I don't want to, Mom. I tried that and look what I got. I don't feel whole if I don't see Cay and the baby for a whole day."

Harriett smiled. Her son was in love. But she knew Max. If he feels like this, he will do anything to combat it. Right now, he views Cayla as Jon's wife. Until he realizes that Jon is really gone and he and Cayla deserve their love, he would always see her that way.

"Well, Son, I suggest you let things happen naturally, see where they take you."

"I haven't spoken to her in three weeks, and it's killing me. Maybe she doesn't want me in their lives. She hasn't called me at all. But you're right, Mom. I can at least see where we go from here. If she rejects the idea of us being in a relationship, I'll have no other alternative but to step out of Cayla's life. I mean romantically, at least, because I will always be a part of my godson's life. That, I will not negotiate on."

Harriett patted his cheek. "You're a good man, Max, and everything will work out."

"Oh yeah, I forgot. Mrs. Sherman is contesting Jon's will," Max told her.

"That doesn't surprise me," she stated.

"Well, I'm fighting it for Cay, but she says she doesn't want the estate for herself. She just wants the Sherman family out of her life."

"Can you blame her? They were horrible to her."

"I know, Mom, but this is her son's inheritance."

"I see your point. Just keep talking to Cayla; she'll come around."

"Cayla is stubborn, Mom."

"And you're not stubborn with a little touch of determination?" his mother asked, smiling.

Max chuckled, still a little unsure.

Chapter Six

Cayla hadn't seen Max since the night they made love. He had arranged for the lawyers to meet at her house, but he didn't come with them. She was told the court served the Sherman's, and they were definitely contesting Jon's will. The lawyers assured her that it would be thrown out. The trust fund for the baby was in place, and no one could touch that. Accounts were opened in her name; although, with the contesting of the will, her assets were frozen. Max, however, had already generously seen to it that she had money at her disposal.

Absently her fingers touched her mouth. She would never forget how good he made her feel. God how she missed him. She knew she was falling in love with Max. At first, she felt guilty because Jon hadn't been gone a year. For propriety's sake, she would keep the love she had for Max to herself. She could admit she loved him because she was honest with herself. Not that she had stopped loving Jon any less. She was sure Jon would understand. Max was her strength. After Jon's death, she thought she would never see or feel happiness ever again. Max made her happy just by being with her, encouraging her, and making her feel she could have a future without Jon. Jon would always be in her heart, and she would make sure his son knew how wonderful his father was. Cayla knew now what she had to do: she could finish her degree, open her business, and make a life for her son and herself. The question that had popped into her head was whether Max felt the same way as she did. When he kissed her, and when he looked at her sometimes, she had thought he did. However, the way she reacted that night he made love to her and after he made her feel so wonderful, she may have ruined any chance she had with him. It was just a week after his making love to her that she may have gotten her answer. He didn't see her, but she saw him. Max and a tall, very attractive woman were walking arm in arm and coming out of the Ritz Carlton. He was smiling at something she was saying. What could Cayla say? He was free to see anyone he chose. She had no ties on him. Hell, she had even encouraged him to date. Maybe it was time for her and the baby to leave, time for her to be on her own. She has become far too dependent on Max. Maybe she needed this space to get over this infatuation she had for him. She made her decision. Cayla now had to tell Max and Harriett that she and the baby would find another place to live after the estate hearing.

Bianca smiled as she left Maxwell's office. She had misjudged her actions with Maxwell. He was not like the men from her past. He was all man. However, she needed to be in control. She would just bide her time. She had to teach him that she was the one in control. She'd play the beta for a while, at least until she had the ring, then all bets were off. Again she had her clutches into Maxwell. After he hadn't contacted her, she went to his office, contrite and apologetic. She told him she was wrong and tried to explain to him why she acted in such a way. Max listened with a half an ear. He told her that she had to learn that he was a man, not some boy or flunky that she could just snap her fingers and he would run to do her bidding - if there was still a relationship. Bianca wanted Max because he was a big man in the corporate world, and he complimented her just as she did him. Her goal was to make them the power couple she knew they could be. They would rule the social set in the upper crust of Atlanta, and she would be the queen, with Maxwell anyway.

Max wasn't sure if he was doing the right thing by taking Bianca back; yet every time he thought about approaching Cayla, he couldn't make himself do it. Other than his mother, Cayla and the baby were the best relationships in his life, and he didn't want to mess that up. He had to stay in his godson's life, so he felt he had to keep combating the feelings he had for Cayla. Bianca was no Cayla, who had an even temperament and sweet personality. Maybe if he introduced Bianca to Cay, let her know that they could never be together, then the attraction for one another would disappear. If Cay knew he was in a relationship, things would right themselves.

****

Harriett had invited Cayla and the baby over for lunch. She wanted the lady known as Nonna to see little Jonathan. Nonna was Max and Jon's godmother. At eighty, she was strong, spry, and the matriarch of the gated community. Everyone knew Nonna. She had raised three sons and two daughters, all now married and with grandchildren of their own. She even had a hand in raising Maxwell and Jonathan. When she learned of Jon's death, Nonna was devastated; Jon was like one of her own children. Then when Harriett told her how Margaret put Jon's young wife out on the street, she was angry. She ordered Harriett to have Cayla and the baby to her house; she wanted to see Jon's child. Of course, Margaret and her daughters wasted no time spreading lies and had everyone believing that the child Cayla carried was not Jon's.

Nonna sat on the sofa across from the mantle, waiting patiently for their arrival.

"Will Maxwell be here as well?" Nonna asked Harriett.

"I told him to come, but I don't think he will. He's trying very hard to stay away from Cayla and the baby. I don't know what's going on with that boy, Nonna. He even went back to that wench I had to throw out of my house for her disrespect. I told you about it," Harriett said.

"You mean that girl that gave you permission to call her by her name?" Nonna laughed.

"Yes, ma'am, that's the one. I had hoped he was done with her, but I think he took back up with her." Harriett rolled her eyes. "But I'm not going to interfere. That boy is fighting a battle within himself."

Harriett leaned forward and whispered, although they were the only two in the room. "Max is in love with Cayla, and he's trying hard not to be. He stopped seeing her and the baby and took up with that wench, thinking he will fall out of love with her."

"Oh please, Ett, what's wrong with him?"

Harriett laughed. "That's what I asked him too."

"Get him on the phone. He'll be here," Nonna said in her gruff manner.

Harriett dialed and handed the phone to Nonna.

"Maxwell, I expect to see you at your mother's for lunch this afternoon and don't disappoint me."

"Nonna?" Max said through the receiver.

"Yes, it's Nonna, so shall I expect you?"

"Yes, ma'am."

"Good." Nonna handed the phone back to Harriett and smiled. "I'll be the judge if he loves her or if she loves him; but more importantly, I want to see that baby."

Cayla pulled into the circular driveway of Max's mother's house. They had become very close since she had given birth. She stayed with her after Jonathan was born. She cared for Cayla as she got stronger and showed her things a young mother wouldn't know. She was most helpful, and Cayla couldn't help but become fond of her. She loved that baby as if she were his blood grandmother. Whenever Harriett would broach the subject of Max, Cayla would cleverly change the subject; therefore, Harriett didn't push.

The air was chilly, so Cayla had the baby wrapped warmly in his carrier. Harriett opened the door and made her way to Cayla and the baby.

"Oh, my goodness," Harriett said, grinning. "Hi, sweetie, let me help you." *That meant give me my baby.* She took the carrier, and Cayla grabbed the diaper bag from the back and followed her into the house. After setting the bag down and removing her coat, Cayla followed Harriett into the living room. Cayla stood in the doorway as she watched Harriett begin to take the baby's outerwear off.

"You think it's warm enough in here, Nonna?" she asked fretfully.

"Oh, it's plenty warm," the older woman answered. "Hurry and finish then bring him to me, Ett. I want to see this baby. Come on in here, child. Let me look at you," Nonna said.

Cayla moved into the room and stood in front of Nonna.

"Do you remember me, child?" she asked sternly.

"Yes, ma'am, you're Jon's godmother," she answered.

"That's right. I saw you at his funeral, and it was like I buried one of my own. Now sit here, child," she said, patting a seat beside her on the sofa. Harriett was busy getting the baby comfortable.

"Now, Cayla, I'm not one to play with words. I say what I say and that's that. Now, is this Jon's son?"

"Yes, ma'am, he is," Cayla said stiffly.

"Bring him here, Harriett," Nonna called over her shoulder. Harriett had placed the baby back in his blanket for a little bit to ensure he was properly warmed from the chill outside. She took the baby to Nonna and placed him in her outstretched hands. Nonna cradled the three-month-old infant in her arms. Gently she loosened the blanket that covered his tiny body. Cayla heard her gasp.

Nonna was looking down at the baby. Tenderness first lit her face, and then tears filled her eyes and rolled down her aged face.

"My Jon is back. Thank you, Jesus, thank you," she said through her tears.

"I told you, Nonna, he looked just as Jon did when he was this age," Harriett said softly.

Nonna looked over at Cayla and took her hand in her aged one, bringing it to her lips.

"Oh, baby, he's beautiful." Cayla smiled.

Just then, his eyes opened, and Nonna started to cry all over again. "Just like my Jonathan. Just look at him, Ett. He has Jonathan's eyes and everything."

"See, Nonna, I told you," Harriett replied, grinning.

Cayla watched as the two women fussed over Jonathan, and she smiled.

Nonna looked over at Cayla. "Now when are we going to have him christened?"

Cayla looked at her, confused. "I hadn't thought about it, ma'am," she answered.

"Call me Nonna, and you best be thinking about it," Nonna replied sternly.

"Well, I guess he should be, but I don't have a church home now, since...."

"And why not? I know for a fact you joined AME Bethel. I was there when you and Jon were together."

"Yes, ma'am, I did, but I haven't been since the funeral."

"You are still a member, and it's your right to attend your church home – right, Ett?"

"Oh yes, Cay. We can choose the date for the christening after we take Jonathan to meet the pastor."

Cayla rose from the sofa and moved to the mantle. Harriett and Nonna looked at each other, frowning.

"Miss Harriett, I have to tell you something," she said softly, looking down at her hands.

"What is it, child?" Nonna asked when she saw the stricken look on Cayla's face.

"I'm thinking of leaving Georgia," she said.

"What?" both women said at the same time.

Harriett went to her, taking her hands in hers. "Why, Cayla? Where will you go?" Harriett asked, alarmed.

Cayla's teary eyes looked at Harriett. "I'm not sure yet. I just can't stay here with the Shermans and…" she paused. "I just can't live here anymore. After I go to court next month, I'll know better where I will go, but I can't stay here. When Mrs. Sherman finds out about Jonathan, she'll think she has a right to him. This will come out in court, I know. Then she'll try and take him away, and under no circumstances will I allow that to happen."

"Honey, don't you worry about Margaret. I'll straighten her behind out," Nonna said.

Harriett looked at Cayla with saddened eyes. "Does Max know how you feel?"

Ms. Harriett didn't know she saw Max with his girlfriend. Cayla didn't want the baby and herself to come between them. She wanted Max to have a life without her interference. "No, I haven't heard from Max in a few weeks," she said, her eyes lowering to study her hands.

Nonna and Harriett studied Cayla. More has gone on between Max and Cayla, and they knew it. Nonna looked at her with eyebrows raised.

"Come here, child. Tell Nonna why you're really running?" Cayla returned to her place beside her.

Nonna took her hand. "Now why are you really leaving?"

Cayla looked into Nonna's wise eyes. "Nonna, there's nothing here for me anymore, and I'll be away from the Shermans. With Jon gone, what's left for me here?"

"You have Max," Harriett stated, looking for a reaction.

Cayla's head lowered. "No, I don't. Max has his own life. He can't always be around to pick up the pieces for me. I must go. I don't want to interfere with Max's life any more than I have. He's been so wonderful to me and the baby, and you don't know how much I appreciate how he took care of me when I was pregnant."

"Well…" Nonna couldn't finish what she wanted to say. Max had arrived.

"Mom! What is Cayla's car doing here…?" Max said, coming into the living room. He stood rooted to the spot when he saw Cayla sitting beside Nonna.

"Max, look who's here," his mother said happily.

Max and Cayla's eyes met and held for a minute. Max's heart leaped in his chest at the sight of her, and his eyes briefly softened before he could stop them.

Nonna and Harriett watched the exchange with interest.

"Hello, Max," Cayla said softly, almost shyly.

"Cayla, what are you doing here?" he asked gruffly. Cayla lowered her head. That wasn't what she expected to hear from him. Obviously, he didn't miss her as much as she missed him.

"I invited her, Maxwell," his mother said brusquely.

"Maxwell, get over here and give me a kiss," Nonna ordered.

"I'm sorry. Hello, Nonna," he said, placing a kiss on her cheek.

Cayla got up from the sofa. "Excuse me," she said softly, leaving the room.

Cayla escaped to the bathroom, closed the door, and leaned on it. She was right. Max had no feelings for her. She should be glad but she was not. She wanted him to miss her as much as she missed him, or at least be happy to see her.

"What is wrong with you, boy?" his mother asked, angered.

"What, Mom?"

"*What are you doing here, Cayla?*" Harriett mimicked him.

"What was I supposed to say, Mom? You know I've been giving us space."

"How about, *Hello, Cayla. How are you and the baby?*" Nonna said. "You're right, Ett. Something's wrong with him."

"Mom, did you tell Nonna?" Max asked incredulously.

"Tell me what?" Nonna asked. "I'm not blind, Max. I can see you have feelings for Cayla. My eyesight has not failed me yet!"

"You're mistaken, Nonna. I don't have feelings for her." He frowned.

"Just by the way you looked at her, I could tell. The eyes are the mirror to the soul, Maxwell," she quoted.

"No disrespect, Nonna, but you're mistaken. I no longer have feelings for her. Of course, I care about her and the baby's welfare; however, I am dating now, and I care about the woman I want to be with." Harriett rolled her eyes at her son and turned away.

Max looked down at the baby in Nonna's arms. God, he missed his son—*he wasn't his son*. He reached out and gently touched the baby's little fist. Nonna lifted the baby to him.

Max took him and inhaled that delicate baby scent. He was lying to himself. He missed his boy. Just because he didn't want to complicate things between him and Cayla, he still could spend time with his godson. He carried him across the room and sat down. He just stared at the baby.

When Cayla returned, Max came to his feet. He looked over at his mother and then went to Cayla.

"I'm sorry, Cay. I was just surprised to see you," he said, handing her the baby.

"It's okay, Max. I understand," she told him as she looked down at her son. The baby started to whimper.

"Is he wet?" Harriett asked, ignoring her son and taking the baby from Cayla. Harriett checked. "He's muddy," she said, chuckling.

"Nonna and I will take care of him. You sit and make yourself comfortable, Cayla. We'll be having lunch as soon I put this little fellow down," she said, leaving the room with the baby and Nonna following behind her. Nonna stopped and narrowed her eyes at Max.

This was the first time Max and Cayla had been alone for a few weeks. Max looked over at her. She had her head down, playing with her fingers.

"What do you understand, Cay?" Max asked after a minute.

Her head rose. "Why did you avoid me, Max?" she asked him instead. "I thought we were at least friends."

Max exhaled. He didn't expect her to ask him that. "What happened between us should have never happened," he stated simply.

Cayla turned away from him.

"You know it's true, Cayla. You said as much."

Cayla faced him. She studied his face for a sign of something to show he cared about her and the baby. "I know I handled things wrong. I shouldn't have reacted like I did, Max. It scared me. I only knew one man in my life, and it scared me the way you made me feel. I'm sorry," Cayla said. She returned to her seat on the sofa. Max stood in front her. He stooped down in front of her.

Eye level with her, Max asked softly. "For what?"

Cayla turned her head. Max caught her chin and turned her to face him.

"For what?" he repeated.

Cayla exhaled. His face was so close to hers. She felt a knot forming in her belly; her pulse pounded.

"I'm sorry I put you in that position, Max." She shrugged. "I don't know. I think we both just got caught up in the moment," she replied softly.

"You do know I care about you and the baby?"

"Then why...?" Cayla paused. She was going to ask him why he stopped coming by. She already knew.

Max rose to his feet and stepped away. "It was wrong what happened, and I'm sorry it did. Jon was my best friend. I feel like I stabbed my best friend in his back," he said angrily.

Cayla looked up at him. His face was hard; his eyes, dark and dangerous. His anger startled her. "I don't want that to happen again," he said.

"It won't," she assured him. "Don't worry, if you want a relationship with Jonathan, you can. I would never stop you from seeing your godson."

Max shook his head. She didn't understand. It was more than just seeing his godson. Max reached out to touch her, but quickly pulled back when he distantly heard Nonna and his mother returning. He moved far away from Cayla.

"We laid the baby on the bed with pillows around him. He'll be fine. Now come on, you two, let's have lunch," Harriett said.

Max and Cayla exchanged looks before she rose and offered to help Harriett.

The lunch was wonderful, and while they ate, Nonna and Harriett planned the baby's christening. They had it planned so well that all Max and Cayla had to do was show up. It would be at the AME Bethel Church in Stone Mountain, and the repast would be held in the church's very large dining room.

Max looked at his mother, who was still a little sour with him for going back to Bianca.

"Are we allowed to bring a guest?" he asked.

Harriett rolled her eyes. "Of course, Maxwell."

"Who you want to bring?" Nonna asked.

"Bianca. She is my lady," he said and glanced over at Cayla. He expected a reaction. When he didn't get one, he was surprised.

Cayla looked over at him and smiled. "I'm glad you're dating, Max," she said.

"You're not surprised?" Max asked her.

"No, I saw you and your lady one day when I was in town. She's very attractive."

"So, you won't mind if I bring her around sometimes when I visit Jonathan?" he asked.

"Why would I mind? She must be special if you chose her."

"She's special all right. The devil incarnate," Harriett muttered.

Cayla turned to talk to Nonna about her offer to be the baby's godmother. Harriett had already said she was the baby's grandmother, and she wanted him to call her Minq.

As the ladies talked, Max couldn't keep his eyes off of Cayla. He thought he would get a reaction from Cayla but not one of indifference. What did he expect? She encouraged him to date, and he was free to do so. So why did it feel so wrong? Regardless of what he was fighting, he wasn't going to let their friendship fall apart because they'd slept together. He wanted to be in that little boy's life, and no one was going to stop him.

Chapter Seven

While driving down the street, a scary thought came to Max. What if Cayla finds love with someone else? Would he be able to handle seeing her with another? This was not the time to be having these thoughts as he pulled his car up to the valet. He was meeting Bianca for dinner, and he was late. She wasn't going to be happy. However, lately she has been less demanding and controlling. Maybe this might work out with Bianca. After entering the restaurant, he could see Bianca sitting at the bar. He could see by her body language that she was not happy. Hell, she had to learn that everything wasn't about her. She needed to understand that he was the man in this relationship, he thought smugly.

The hostess returned and offered to get Bianca from the bar. He went to the table and stood beside it. Bianca's face was tight with anger, and he could see the annoyance on it as she followed the hostess.

Max stood behind her chair. When she sat, he bent over to kiss her, but she turned her face away.

"Sorry, babe, time got away from me." He took his seat across from her. After taking Nonna home, he stopped by Cayla's house. He was in luck because baby Jonathan was still awake, and he spend the last few hours with his godson. It appeared that everything was back on track between him and Cayla, and they talked just like old friends. She even laughed at his plans for Jonathan's future. The estate hearing was in a couple of days, and he assured her that everything would be alright. He had to attend the hearing, so he could testify on Jon and Cayla's behalf. All he knew was he had his friend's back, and that made him smile. Before he knew it, it was five o'clock, and he was supposed to meet Bianca for dinner at six o'clock.

Bianca turned to him. "Where were you? You know I don't like to be kept waiting, Maxwell," she pouted.

He had to let her know about Cayla and his godchild. If they were going to be together, it was her right to know. Plus, he wasn't hiding his relationship with his godson from anyone. Bianca had to know how important the baby was to him.

"I went to see my godson," he answered.

"Godson? You kept me waiting because of some kid?" she asked incredulously.

Max lay down the menu. He didn't appreciate her tone. "Let's get something straight, Bianca. That little boy means the world to me. He is the son of my best friend, who just a year ago died, and I promised him *and* myself that I would be in his son's life. Is there a problem with that?"

Bianca swallowed her retort. "What about the mother?"

"We are friends, and one day soon you will meet both of them. They are important to me, and if we are still in a relationship, it is important that you accept that they will be in my life."

"How old is the baby?" she asked.

Max smiled. "He's just six months."

Bianca sighed. This little tidbit he just laid on her was going to complicate things for her, or maybe not. She had no intentions of having any children; maybe this could work in her favor. "Okay, honey."

"So, we're good?"

"Of course."

Max opened his menu, showing the discussion was over. He didn't want to get into an argument with Bianca in this crowded restaurant and was surprised she didn't put up much of an argument. He could feel her eyes boring into his forehead, right through the leather-bound menu. He had a feeling this was not over.

Bianca glared at the back of the leather-bound menu. These past few weeks with him were slowly draining the control she craved from her soul. She needed to get it back, and that wouldn't happen until he put that ring on her finger. Her eyes were cold and hard with bitterness, and they darkened with a ruthless determination.

Max lowered the menu and met her eyes. However, he had missed the fury burning hot and wild in them. He lifted an eyebrow with that no-nonsense look about him that said he was accustomed to taking charge. "Are you ready to order, Bianca?" he asked.

Dark lashes half-lowered over her eyes, and then she lifted them with a sweet demure smile that masked her fury before she nodded.

****

Cayla checked her face in the rearview mirror and took a nervous breath. She was meeting Maxwell at the courthouse for the estate hearing. If it were not for her son, she would let Mrs. Sherman have it all. However, for her son she would do anything. In her heart, she knew Jon approved. He may not have known his son, but he loved him the minute she told him that she carried his child. "Oh, Jon, it's at times like this that I miss you so much," she whispered, closing her eyes to stem the tears that filled them. "We made a beautiful boy, and he looks just like you." The tears she didn't want to shed rolled down her face. Quickly she pulled a tissue from her purse and dabbed at her eyes. She couldn't go into court looking like a raccoon. Once again, she checked her face before getting out of the car. She glanced at her watch. She was early for the proceedings, but she needed that time to get herself together emotionally. The last thing she wanted was to run into Mrs. Sherman and her evil daughters, the wicked witches of the southeast.

Max had phoned last night to encourage her and to tell her not to worry. He said that Mark Rodgers, her lawyer, was the best at what he did. That was reassuring.

After hanging up with him, she thought about his saying that he was dating exclusively. She was happy for him. Plus, it was a good way to forget about their little indiscretion. She shouldn't let it bother her so much. She was happy for Max. He was a good guy, and he deserved someone he could love. The anniversary of Jon's death was fast approaching, and she had to go to his grave. She hadn't been since the day of his funeral, but it was time to let go. She had her son to raise and a life to get on with, and she was going to do that. Jon would want her to be happy - that much she was sure of.

She lifted her head and looked up at the Fulton County Courthouse. She grabbed the handrail and climbed the steep stairs to the place that would decide if she was worthy of being respected as Jonathan Sherman's wife.

"Cayla!" She stopped and looked over her shoulder when she heard her name called. It was Max and Mark. Both men looked like GQ in their expensive suits. Even the briefcase Mark carried looked expensive.

She lifted her hand and waved, waiting for them on the landing. She had to admit, they were two fine looking men. Mark Rodgers was good looking but not as handsome as Maxwell. Mark was married and was about to become a father himself. He was a good man. He also reassured her that she had nothing to worry about. Everything, he had told her, was rightly hers and Jon's son.

"Hi, Cay," Max greeted and kissed her cheek. Mark shook her hand.

"Are you ready?" Mark asked, smiling.

"I guess so," she said softly. The three of them continued up the concrete steps, and Max held the door as she preceded the men into the courthouse.

Max walked beside her. "You look pretty, Cay," Max complimented.

She smiled and looked over at Max. "Thank you, Max."

She sure hoped so. It took her an hour to find the right outfit to wear to court. The navy suit and white blouse, she hoped, was appropriate for a hearing. She had her hair pulled back and only wore a simple pair of faux diamond stud earrings along with her wedding ring. She was lucky she was wearing them when she was thrown out of the condo. Of course, she had plenty of good jewelry that Jon had given her as gifts, but all of it was in the hands of Mrs. Sherman.

She looked down at her hands, rubbing the rings where they rested on her finger for strength.

"Wait here, guys," Mark said. "I'm going to talk to the bailiff to see how long we have to wait." Mark went through the double doors.

Max was having a hard time keeping his eyes off Cayla. She looked so pretty and so nervous. How he wished he could take that apprehension from her. He wished a lot of things, but they were not meant to be.

"How's Jon?" he asked to keep his thoughts on simple things and not on how much he wanted Cayla to be his.

"He's good. Your mom has him. He slept fitfully last night. Poor baby cried most of the night. I wanted to take him to the emergency room, but I called your mom when I couldn't think of why he was crying.

"She told me he was probably teething and told me to rub his little gums. That seemed to help. He stopped crying and went to sleep. Early this morning, I got some baby Orajel, and he's fine now. You have to come by and see the little tooth trying to break through his gums." She smiled and his heart jumped in his chest.

"I have a meeting after this, but I'll stop by Mom's later."

"Hey, guys, we're up," Mark said, coming out of the courtroom. He stood in front of Cayla. "Cayla, Mrs. Sherman and her daughters are already inside. If she says anything to you, just ignore her, okay?"

"I have no problem with that, Mark," she stated and pulled open the door to the courtroom with Max and Mark behind her.

Mark led her to the defendant's table, and Max took a seat behind them. The judge presiding over this case had not arrived. Mark placed his briefcase on the table and pulled out a file then took the seat beside her. He was ready to put these hateful people in their place.

Margaret Sherman looked over at Cayla. It would be over her dead body if that strumpet took her son's estate. There was nothing in the world that was going to stop her from keeping that gold digger's hands off her son's money. When she got done disparaging her character, no judge in the state of Georgia will award her a piece of dirt. Margaret was having a hard time not voicing her opinion. Her lawyer told her to be quiet. Her personal family lawyer told her she didn't have a case. She fired him. Stanley Bennet, her new lawyer, was a little sleazy and a lot greedy. He also told her that her case was weak, but he took her case because the money was right. He had given her some suggestions that could possibly place the case to her advantage. She took the advice and ran with it. She produced photos of Cayla with different men. They were fake, of course; her daughters were very good with photoshop. When she was going through Cayla and Jon's things, she found a few pictures of Cayla and Jon, and they were easy to manipulate. She had meant to get rid of the despicable photos of her son with that woman, but she was now glad that she still had them. It was at least five pictures, each in various places and times, but with some random man's face that the girls found online to complete the sabotage. Technology is a beautiful thing.

"What is taking the judge so long," she whispered to her lawyer.

"Mrs. Sherman, please be quiet. You have to look like the grieving mother trying to save her son's estate. So do be quiet. The judge will enter when he is ready."

Mrs. Sherman rolled her eyes. "Just be sure you have the evidence to ruin her," she mumbled.

Cayla ignored the comments coming from her ex-sisters-in-law from across the aisle, but Max quickly became sick of it. They were not trying to curb the loud comments for all to hear. Max rose, and Cayla watched as he moved toward them.

Max leaned over and, in a low tone, replied, "Ladies, I trust your mother has raised you with a bit of decorum. Let's try and use it. If I hear another disparaging remark coming from this side of the aisle, my next action will be a legal one."

Both women's mouths dropped open. Mrs. Sherman turned in her seat. "You dare to correct my daughters when you are consorting with a gold digger? You should be ashamed, Maxwell. You and Jonathan were like brothers, and I am so disappointed in you for taking that woman's side. She is beneath us all." Margaret shook her head. "Umph, well I guess if you lay down in the gutter long enough, some of that filth is going to grow on you."

"With all due respect, Mrs. Sherman, I will not dignify your implications and remarks. But just so you know, every word that comes from you and your daughters' mouths is recorded. Slander is an ugly thing, Mrs. Sherman." Max turned and walked away, with the Shermans staring at him.

"Is that true?" she asked her lawyer.

He leaned in close to Mrs. Sherman. "I have warned you. Your case is weak, but you insist on doing these unwise things. As I suggested before, be quiet - and your daughters as well."

"All rise. The Honorable Judge Harold M. Cowell presiding.

"Remain standing," the bailiff ordered after the judge sat. "Since this is a small group, I will swear all of you in at once. Raise your hand. *Do you swear that the evidence that you shall give shall be the truth, the whole truth and nothing but the truth, so help you God?*"

After the collective, *"I do"* was heard, the judge told them to be seated. Judge Cowell explained the rules and respect he wanted in the courtroom. He asked the attorneys to give their opening statements. Attorney Bennett gave his statement, and then Mark approached the front of the courtroom and gave his opening statement of the case. It was then time for the opposing attorney to present his case. He started with saying that Cayla's marriage to Jonathan Sherman was invalid. His next statement had Mark, Cayla and Max stunned. Opposing counsel alleged that Cayla was seen out on the town just days after Jonathan's death and stated they had proof. Cayla turned around and looked at Max. He could see the anger simmering in her eyes. Beside her, Mark could sense the anger in her and whispered, "Stay calm."

"Objection, Your Honor. No foundation established. Where is the proof?" Mark said.

"I have proof, Your Honor, but it has not yet arrived," Bennet replied.

"Objection sustained. Mr. Bennet, don't test my patience. Did you go to some law school that taught you to make claims without providing simultaneous evidence?" the judge asked sternly.

"No, Your Honor, I apologize. However, I do reserve the right to revisit this subject at a later time."

"So noted; move on, Counselor."

After Stanley finished presenting and sat down, Mark called Maxwell Washington to the stand.

Max went to the stand and was reminded that he was under oath. Mark asked him various questions about his relationship to Jonathan, his role as witness, and his observations of Jonathan and Cayla's marriage. Max answered all questions and stated clearly what Jonathan had disclosed as his wishes for his family. Satisfied, Mark turned the questioning over to Stanley, who declined. Cayla was called to the stand next. Her lawyer asked, "Mrs. Sherman, can you tell us how you and Jonathan Sherman met?" She smiled gently before she told them how she and Jon met, about the whirlwind marriage in Las Vegas, and how happy they were.

"Your honor, in your file of this case, you will find the authenticated marriage license – Exhibit C," he reminded the judge. "Now, Mrs. Sherman, please tell the court about the incident that resulted in you being homeless."

Cayla looked directly at Margaret Sherman when she told the court how Margaret evicted her from the home she and Jonathan shared, just a month after her husband's death.

"She is a liar!" Margaret shouted, coming to her feet. Stanley pulled her back into her seat.

"Counselor, you will restrain your client. I will not tolerate any outburst in my courtroom, is that understood?" Judge Cowell replied tersely.

"Yes, Your Honor," he said meekly.

"Do you have any questions for Mrs. Sherman?" the judge asked Stanley after Mark finished.

He stood and approached the witness stand. It was an intimidating tactic some lawyers used. "Mrs. Sherman, you say that you and Jonathan Sherman had a happy relationship?"

"Yes, we did," she answered.

"Did you know that your alleged husband took up with a mistress after he married you? If you were so happy, why do you think he had to have one?"

Cayla chuckled. "Where did you get that information, Mr. Bennett?"

"I'm asking the questions, Mrs. Sherman. Did you know Jonathan Sherman had a mistress?" he demanded.

"No, I did not, because he didn't have a mistress," she answered simply.

"If this is true, Counselor, where is this said mistress?" the judge asked Stanley, who began fidgeting and pulling at the collar of his shirt. "We could not locate her, Your Honor," he answered.

Judge Cowell's eyes narrowed. "The evidentiary rules of the court apply to you as well, Mr. Bennet, and so do contempt charges if you persist with this tactic, Counselor!"

"Yes, Your Honor," Stanley said before continuing.

"You allege that Mrs. Sherman evicted you from your home without your property. Is it not true that she offered to have your property taken to a storage, paying for a year's rent until you could get them."

"I did say she offered to have them stored. It was my choice not to accept her offer. That was a mistake on my part. I don't blame anyone for decisions I've made."

"So now you want to claim the estate of a man who may not legally be your husband. No further questions." Stanley turned and took his seat, and Cayla stepped from the stand.

Mark then rose and called for Mrs. Margaret Sherman to take the stand. The stately woman rose and took her seat in the witness stand. Mark sent a barrage of questions her way. Some she could answer; others, she stammered over. It wasn't long before Mrs. Sherman got frustrated with Mark's line of questioning.

"She is a whore and gold digger. She has tainted the Sherman name. Look at her. She's not even good enough to be my son's widow. She's nothing but ghetto trash… the little hussy."

The judge banged his gavel, calling for order and demanding that Mrs. Sherman re-take her seat.

Judge Cowell cleared his throat. "I have heard all I need to hear. If there is nothing further the court needs to consider, I'm ready to rule."

Stanley and Mrs. Sherman pushed a file back and forth to each other before Stanley called over the bailiff and handed him the folder, which he gave to the judge.

"Your Honor, that is the evidence to support our earlier claim regarding Cayla Sherman's character," Stanley said.

The judge opened the folder and looked at the contents. The judge closed the folder and told the bailiff to take it to Mr. Rodgers.

"Mr. Rodgers, did you know of this new evidence that Mr. Bennet just presented to the court?"

Mark opened the folder and surveyed the contents. He showed it to Cayla. She gasped and had to cover her mouth to keep from laughing. It wasn't even a good photoshop job.

"Mrs. Sherman, is that you in those photos?" the judge asked.

Cayla rose. "Yes, Your Honor, it is me, but I don't know those men. You can probably find them on any stock photo site on the web," she said. "Whoever did this did a horrible job of manipulation, if you ask me." She retook her seat.

"I agree," the judge said. "Let's get on with this, please. First, I have looked over the documents presented by both counselors, and I have to say this was a waste of my time and tax dollars." He addressed Mrs. Sherman.

"Mrs. Sherman, I am sorry for the loss of your son; however, you have no case. Jonathan changed his will a week after he and your daughter-in-law wed. The will and power of attorney that you presented became null and void when your son changed his will, and it was signed by his witness, Maxwell Washington. Also, powers of attorney are voided once a person expires. You will return all of Mrs. Sherman's possessions, the condo and all the cars. Your son has left you very well-off, Mrs. Sherman. Be happy with what you have. The bulk of the estate goes to his wife, Cayla Sherman, and his son, Jonathan Thomas Sherman II, in addition to the trust for said son."

The three Sherman women across the aisle were on their feet. "My son did not impregnate that woman. That kid is not my son's," Margaret shouted at the judge.

"Do sit down, ladies," the judge ordered tersely.

"Again, Mrs. Sherman, you are wrong. I have the DNA results here, and they say Jonathan Thomas Sherman II is 99.99999% his son. I'm ready to rule," the judge replied. He read what Cayla and her son were entitled to, not counting the things that Mrs. Sherman was ordered to return to her. Cayla was now a very wealthy woman.

The judge officially ended the hearing. Cayla rose and hugged Mark, thanking him. She turned to a grinning Max. Her eyes misted as she smiled. "Is it really over?" she asked.

Max pulled her into his arms and hugged her tight. He hadn't felt her in his arms in a very long time and damn did it feel good. Her scent was like heaven. He finally had to push away because things were happening where they shouldn't be. He looked at his watch.

"Hey, how about we go get our boy and take him to lunch to celebrate?"

Cayla smiled. It sounded good with him calling Jonathan "our boy."

"That's a great idea. Maybe your mom will join us."

Mark said his goodbyes. He was late for lunch with his wife. Max and Cayla turned to exit the courtroom.

"Cayla," Margaret Sherman shouted.

Cay tensed, but she respectfully turned to address the woman. Margaret strolled up the aisle toward them with her daughters bringing up the rear. Margaret stopped in front of Cayla and Max.

"You think you've won," she said, looking Cayla up and down.

"According to Judge Cowell, I have won. If you have something to say, Mrs. Sherman, I'd appreciate it if you'd get on with it, please." Max was proud of her. Cay was nobody's punk, he was beginning to see.

"Don't you take that tone with my mother," Sherri snapped.

"Then tell your mother to get on with it," Cay said back.

"Bitch…"

"Sherri, you will calm yourself. You were not raised in the gutter, like others I know. Just because you swindled my son out of the estate doesn't make you better than me," Margaret said through gritted teeth.

"No, Mrs. Sherman, it does not, and I am not going to stand here and exchange barbs with you. If you have something to say, please get on with it," Cayla insisted. She could feel Max's hand on the small of her back, and he just didn't know how his touch made her strong.

"I want to see my grandson," Mrs. Sherman blurted out.

Cay frowned. "Not the one you claimed was not your son's child? You couldn't by chance be speaking of *that* child?"

"It is my right."

"No, Mrs. Sherman, it is not. Over the past few years, you have told anyone that would listen to you how much you despised me and how I was after Jon's money. Just so you know, Mrs. Sherman, Jon and I were very much in love. Before he died, he knew I carried his child. The only thing I hate is that he never got to meet his son. As far as I'm concerned, you have forfeited your right to anything that is in my life. However…"

Margaret Sherman's upper lip turned up as if she smelled something rotten. "You will bring my grandson to me or risk losing him. I will sue you for custody. I will use every resource that I have to take Jon's son from you."

"Be careful, Mrs. Sherman," Max warned.

"It's okay, Max," she said calmly. "See, Mrs. Sherman, I am sensitive to your feelings. After all, you lost your son just as I lost my husband. I was going to allow you to see my baby, but as usual, you have placed your foot in your mouth. Let me warn you so that we are crystal clear. If you try to take my son, you will know what hell on earth means because I will bring the hounds of hell upon you. Have a wonderful day." She smiled before she turned and left the three-stunned women staring after her.

Chapter Eight

Bianca was walking up the sidewalk and texting Max. She had been calling and texting him since she came out of her ten o'clock meeting. Her calls went to voicemail, and her text messages went unanswered. Now she was pissed. After sending the last text, she dropped the phone in her purse. She was just about to walk into The Bistro, when she saw Max sitting at a table near the window. If she was angry then, her half Latin blood began to boil now. She was ready to explode. She couldn't believe he was sitting there with his horrible mother and another woman, and they were laughing it up as he played with the baby in his arms. That must be the godson he mentioned, and somebody's baby's momma with him. The important thing is that he should have talked to her before he arranged this little gathering without her. Bianca took a breath and entered The Bistro. She didn't bother to stop and walked right past the hostess podium with the young girl chasing after her.

Max lifted his head after blowing on the side of the giggling baby's neck to see Bianca striding irately toward their table. No, he was not going to do this here in front of his mother and Cayla. He handed the baby to Cayla and rose. He wanted to intercept Bianca, because if she came out her mouth wrong, Harriett Washington was going to mop the floor with her.

Max cursed silently. He was too late, and Bianca was glaring at Cayla and the baby. She hadn't even addressed his mother, which would be the respectful thing to do.

She looked over at him and smiled a smile that didn't reach her eyes. "Well, well, Max, I see you are having lunch already. I have been calling all morning to see if we could have lunch together. But I see you had already made arrangements - arrangements that you didn't have the foresight to tell me about."

Max excused himself and took Bianca's arm. She pulled away from him. "Aren't you going to introduce me to your family?" she asked snidely. Her eyes met Harriett's.

"Don't bother with me. We have already met," Harriett said with a fake smile of her own. Harriett was honest in her dislike of Bianca. She looked at her son and shook her head.

Max cleared his throat. He was silently simmering. He had to decide soon just how far he was willing to take their relationship.

"Bianca, this is Cayla Sherman, and this is Jonathan." Max smiled at the baby who was reaching up to him.

"Oh, how sweet," she hissed before turning away. Cayla's eyebrows rose. Max excused himself and then followed her.

"Wow," Cayla said.

Harriett looked at the couple with disgust. "That's his girlfriend. Remind me to tell you about my first meeting with the devil's handmaiden, little Miss Bianca."

"She's very pretty," Cay commented.

"All that glitters ain't gold, honey. Oh, yeah, now tell me about Mrs. Sherman's theatrics in court."

Bianca stood in The Bistro's now-empty waiting area. She was looking out of the plate glass window. She was so angry, she could scream. She was losing control over Maxwell, and she was not happy. Her thoughts went back to the time when she first met Maxwell Washington. *She noticed him when he first walked into the restaurant. He was absolutely beautiful. Tall, built and had a swagger that could turn many women's heads. She immediately sensed the power the fine African-American man exuded. As he walked into the room, he was greeted with* respect and friendly banter. He sat at a vacant booth at the back of the area close to the bar. While she had dinner, she kept her eyes on him. He was tossing drink after drink down his throat. At one point, she thought she saw tears rolling down his face. Her waitress brought her the check.

"Excuse me. Who is that?" she asked the server. She looked over to where Bianca indicated and grinned.

"That is the fine Mr. Maxwell Washington. He's a nice man," she added.

"What do you know about him?" Bianca asked her.

"Well, he is one of Atlanta's richest African-American residents. He has one of the best architectural firms in the state. He practically designed and built most of the buildings in Buckhead and the surrounding areas. The list is too long. It's even rumored that he's being considered to be a candidate for Mayor next year. At least that is what the city of Atlanta wants. He's highly revered and respected in the community. Any woman that hooks him will be one of the most powerful in the city. I know he'd get my vote," she snickered.

"So he's single."

Bianca signed the check and continued to stare at Max with a small smile on her lips. Yes, just the type of man she was looking for. When she got done with him, it wouldn't be a rumor. It will be a fact, and she will be the First Lady of Atlanta. Fluffing her long hair, she went to his booth. She was determined to go in for the kill. She coyly cleared her throat. "Want some company?" she asked demurely.

Bianca huffed. This was not going her way at all. Maxwell had to be devoted to her and only her, not his horrible mother or that brat and its mother. She had to come at him another way, if she was going to be his wife one day soon. Whenever she wanted to talk about the rumor of him running for mayor, he would change the subject. If she didn't want this so bad, she would drop him quick, but he was everything she needed. He was good-looking, intelligent, popular and well respected. She had met a few of his friends, some added up; others—it would be no hardship to get rid of them. Her problem now is his mother, that kid and its mother. She had to really think things through, so she could pull Max away from them and into her web. Bianca sighed. *But how?* She had worked hard throughout her life to get what she wanted. Now that she was where she wanted to be and her dreams were just within her grasp, no one was going to stop her - and she meant no one.

Max saw Bianca standing by the window; however, he took a few minutes to try to calm himself before approaching her. Unfortunately, it didn't work as well as he'd hoped.

"Bianca!" Max's deep voice snapped behind her.

She rolled her eyes and slowly turned. "How could you do this to me, Max?" she asked with tears glistening in her eyes.

Max frowned. "What is it that you think I've done to you, Bianca?" he asked impatiently.

"I've been trying to call you all morning, and then I find you having lunch with some woman and your mother. How do you think I felt, Maxwell?" she sniffed.

Max reached into his pocket and looked at the phone. He had forgotten to turn his phone back on after they left court.

Max sighed and moved closer. "I'm sorry, baby." He pulled her into his arms.

Bianca pushed away. "I thought we were going to make this relationship work," she pouted. "Don't you want that?"

"Bianca, I do, but you have to give me room to breathe. I do have a life outside us."

That was not what Bianca wanted to hear. She was his priority, and he needed to learn that. Maybe she needed to teach him a lesson. "Okay, fine, Maxwell. When you find the time for me, give me a call." She turned and walked out of The Bistro.

Maxwell squeezed the bridge of his nose before re-joining his family at the table.

*****

Cayla, Harriett and Nonna arrived at church services as the congregation was filling the pews. The day of Little Jonathan's christening came swiftly. Cayla sat in the Washington family pew along with her family, while Nonna sat with her son, daughter, grandchild and great grands. It was a wonderful sight to see. Nonna was greatly admired by all in the church, but the love of her family radiated from them like the brightest sunshine. She also noticed that Harriett kept looking back at the door then at her watch. Services were going to start soon, and Max still hadn't arrived.

"Ms. Harriett," Cayla said, placing her hand on hers. "He'll be here."

"Yes, honey, he will. It's just not like him to be late for services. I think I know what's keeping him, but I'm in church and will just call the devil a liar." Harriett looked over at the sleeping baby in the carrier. When they first arrived, several people stopped them to get a look at Jon's son. Word spread like fire that Jonathan Sherman had a son, and everyone was curious about the young widow and the baby. Harriett just hoped that woman of Maxwell's didn't talk him out of coming.

Cayla's only worry was Mrs. Sherman. She didn't want to have another confrontation with her and her daughters. Mrs. Sherman would not show her true colors in front of others. She was a stickler for keeping up appearances.

The congregation stood as the choir marched in singing the song that opened the service. Once the large choir stood in the choir pit, the pastor stood to the pulpit for opening prayer and the reading of the verse. After everyone was seated, the service began.

Cayla and Harriett smiled to see that, with all the loud singing and praising of the Lord, Little Jonathan continued to sleep. They looked over to see Maxwell coming in the side entrance with Bianca. She didn't look very happy to be in attendance.

Harriett and Cayla moved down on the pew to make room for the late arrivals. Harriett glanced at Max. He shrugged. "Sorry, Mom," he mouthed. Harriett nodded and turned her attention to the word.

Bianca sat beside Cayla. "Good Morning," Cayla whispered. Bianca looked down her nose at her but tipped her head. Cayla looked around her at Max. "You in trouble," she whispered.

Max grinned at her. "I know," he whispered back.

"Do you mind?" Bianca hissed under her breath.

"Excuse me," Cayla replied.

Max leaned to Bianca. "You better behave. Don't embarrass me in front of my church family," he whispered in her ear.

Max shook his head, thinking about the drama he had when he went to pick up Bianca. First, she wasn't ready, and secondly, she told him she wasn't sure she wanted to go. He told her that was fine and turned to leave. She quickly got dressed, complaining the entire time. It gave him time to wonder again if being in a relationship with Bianca was good for his mental health. Anyway, his using Bianca to keep his feelings for Cayla at bay wasn't working. Every time he saw Cayla, he just wanted to take her in his arms and tell her how he felt about her.

Max glanced over at Cay. She looked so pretty with her hair loose, which she seldom did. He smiled when he heard the baby mewling in the carrier. Harriett reached in the carrier and lifted the baby, handing him to Cay. She rose to leave the pew. Max leaned around Bianca. "Is he okay?" Max asked softly.

"He's fine. He just needs to be fed and changed." Harriett smiled when Bianca nudged Max to sit back.

Cayla had just tucked her breast in and was lifting the baby over her shoulder to burp him when the door to the nursery opened. She turned to see Mrs. Sherman and her daughters behind her. Mrs. Sherman's eyes instantly went to the baby in her arms. Cayla took a step back.

"We want to see that baby," Sherri demanded, taking a step toward Cayla. Her mother's arm came out to block her.

"We are in church," her mother hissed. "Yes, Cayla. I want to see him—please?" Mrs. Sherman asked.

Cayla frowned. She didn't know this woman. Mrs. Sherman had never said a kind word to her.

"Why? You don't believe that he's Jon's son," Cayla countered. "However, this is not the place to get into a debate about it, so yes, you may see him," Cayla nodded. Not once did she take her eyes off them. Jonathan took that moment to burp. Cay smiled, lifted the baby from her shoulder and wiped his mouth with the corner of the blanket. She cradled him in her arms and stepped closer to Mrs. Sherman so she could see her grandson.

Margaret's eyes filled and her hand covered her mouth. "He looks just like my Jon," she said, awed.

"Mom, that's Jon," the two behind her said as they stared at the baby.

"He's beautiful," Margaret said and touched his tiny hand. "Can I hold him?"

Cay stepped away from them and laid the baby on the layette in the nursery. She began to change him for the christening. "I have to prepare him for the christening."

Before Margaret left, she asked. "Did Jon know about him?"

Cayla looked over her shoulder. "I told you in court that he did, and he was very happy about the pregnancy."

Margaret's eyes narrowed on Cayla as she turned her back. She had everything: her son's estate and now his child. There was no way she was going to let Cayla keep her out of her grandson's life. She had to bide her time. There were too many people milling around for her to demand that Cayla allow her in her grandson's life.

Max kept looking back at the door Cayla had gone through. Bianca looked over at him.

"What are you looking at?" she hissed quietly.

Max looked at her and rose, ignoring her question. He walked to the back of the church and went to the nursery. He could hear voices coming through the door. He rapped on the door and opened it.

Right away he got an attitude and was just about to voice it.

"It's okay, Max. Mrs. Sherman just wanted to see the baby," Cayla said quickly.

Margaret looked over at Max. "He looks just like Jon when he was that age," she said, her tone strained.

"Yes, he does."

Margaret looked at Cayla. "I want to be in his life. As his grandmother, it is my right, and you cannot deny me," she snapped, reverting back to her nastiness.

"Mrs. Sherman, this is not the place for this debate. He will be getting christened today, and you are more than welcome to stay for the ceremony. I will not discuss what rights you have today."

"Who do you think you are talking too?" Sherri barked.

Max went to the door and held it open. "If it were me, I would not have extended that invitation after the things you have done, so let's not ruin Jonathan's christening and embarrass yourselves."

Sherri opened her mouth to reply, but her mother pulled her by the arm and they left.

Max looked down at the wiggling and cooing baby. "Hey, Little Man," Max greeted, taking his foot and kissing it. "You okay?" he asked Cayla.

"I'm good. I do believe Mrs. Sherman was surprised," Cay commented as she finished dressing the baby.

Max nodded. "Are you sure you want her at the ceremony?"

Cay shrugged. "Max, she lost her son too. I won't go so far as to say I want her in Jonathan's life, but shouldn't he know that she is his grandmother?"

Max shook his head. "You have a good heart, Cayla Sherman," he said and kissed her on the forehead.

Cayla's cheeks heated as she looked at him. She ignored the fast beat of her heart and finished getting the baby ready for the ceremony.

"He looks beautiful," Max said as he took pictures of the baby with his phone.

Cayla handed him to Max as she gathered her bag. She watched as Max and the baby bonded. Tears filled her eyes. She was really missing Jon today, and with the anniversary of his death so close, she was really feeling melancholy. She turned away when hot tears slipped down her face.

Max frowned. "Cay, what's wrong?" he asked.

"Oh, Max, I miss him so much. He should be here."

Max was ashamed of himself, but he was jealous of his best friend. He put his free arm around Cayla and hugged her into his side.

"I'd like to believe that he is here, and he is smiling down on you and his son."

Cayla laid her head on his chest. "I'd like to believe that too." She looked up at him with a wavering smile.

All Max could think was how much he wanted to kiss her sadness away. The moment passed when Jonathan reached over and grabbed his mother's curls.

"Hey, sweet boy," she cooed as she took his hand and kissed it.

"We better go. Service will be ending soon," Max said.

Max carried the baby, and he had Cayla's hand in his as they returned to the pew. He handed the baby to Cayla and went to sit beside Bianca.

"Where were you?" she said. Max decided she was not going to ruin his mood today.

After the service was over, Cayla was crowded by the parishioners of the church, wanting to see the baby.

The church dining hall was decorated with blue and white, even Jon's carrier was covered with blue and white blankets as the camera flashed. Nonna and Harriett had the festivities catered and served, and even a professional photographer was hired for the pictures.

Bianca was getting sick of it all. She stood in back of the hall as Godmother Nonna and honorary Grandmother Harriett stood on either side of Cayla and Max while they held the baby for photographs.

"Ms. Harriett, I think we should have a photo of Mrs. Sherman and her daughters with Jonathan," Cayla said.

"Honey, that's up to you," she smiled.

"Mrs. Sherman, would you like to have a photo of you and the baby?" Cayla called.

Margaret was shocked by the question, but she didn't hesitate to join them. Cayla handed her the baby and moved out of the way as her daughters joined them.

Max was standing beside Nonna. "Cayla has a good heart," she said to him.

Max smiled. "Yes, Nonna, she does."

"So, why are you with that woman over there who's looking like she'd rather be anywhere but here." Nonna's eyebrows lifted as she looked at Max.

Max had totally forgotten about Bianca. He leaned over and kissed Nonna's cheek before rushing over to kiss his mother. "Mom, I have to go. I'll talk to you later."

Harriett shook her head and watched Bianca fuss as they walked out of the door.

"He's not going to take much more of her," Harriett commented.

"Excuse me," Cay said and walked away.

Chapter Nine

Cayla pushed the stroller up the walkway to Jon's gravesite. She still couldn't believe it had already been a year. She still cried for him as if it were yesterday. If it weren't for the baby and Max, she would have lost her mind a while ago. Max was wonderful. He came at least three times a week to spend time with the baby. She smiled each time at the way Jonathan would light up when he saw him. This gave her the opportunity to search out her future. She was going to open the design business she had always wanted. She had even reached out to the people whose homes she had done while she was still in school. She only had a few credits to get, and she would complete her degree. She hadn't spoken to Max about her plans yet. She was kind of afraid that he would scoff at her plans and dreams. She would talk to him anyway. After all, this was her life.

Cayla turned the corner to see someone already standing over Jon's grave. As she got closer, she could see that it was Maxwell. His shoulders sagged as he looked down. Once she was closer, she called out his name.

He turned, and she could see him wipe his face before he smiled. He met them halfway.

"Hello, Cay," he greeted before he lifted the excited baby from the stroller. "I see we had the same thoughts." He turned and walked away. Cay could hear him talking to Jonathan about his father, and she smiled. After they stood there for a minute, Max gave her privacy with Jon.

Cay took a deep breath. "I miss you, Jon," she said. "We have a beautiful son, and I wish you were here.

"I am doing okay. If it weren't for Max, I don't know where I'd be. Wow, you and I had some amazing times, Babe. Thank you for bringing such joy into my life. Yeah, it's been tough without you, but I'm trying to get stronger every day, especially for our son. Okay, okay... I was never a punk, so somehow, I'll get through. I *have* been thinking about my next step, and if it's alright with you, baby, I think it's time for me to move forward with my life. I want to accomplish the things you and I talked about. I want to make you and our son proud of me. Most of all, Jon, I will always love you, and I want to thank you for taking care of us." Cayla brushed tears from her face. She turned away to see Max holding the baby high as he giggled down at him. Cayla joined them, and together they left the cemetery.

    Max helped them into the car. He watched as they drove away. His heart was telling him that he needed to be with Cayla. He didn't miss the tear tracks on her face. If he did go to her, what could he do to comfort a woman in love with a dead man? He couldn't compete with that. Max let out a sigh and decided he was doing the right thing by continuing his relationship with Bianca. She recently heard that he had been approached to run for mayor of Atlanta, and now she has become a broken record about it. Max shook his head. Bianca was trying her best to convince him to run, and so were others in his inner circle. Now, he was even considering it.

*****

    "Where are we going?" Bianca asked when they missed the turn off to his mother's house. They were due for dinner, and Bianca was making a concerted effort to get along with his mom. His mother wasn't budging on her dislike of Bianca, and he couldn't blame her. He knew why Bianca was willing to make amends to his mother: she has her eyes on being First Lady of Atlanta. He hadn't even made a decision about it, nor had he spoken to his mother.

    He glanced at her. "I thought I'd stop by and see my godson, since it's on the way."

Bianca rolled her eyes. "Please, Maxwell, I'm not in the mood for some brat," she snipped.

Max put on his blinker, pulled to the side of the road and put the car in park. He turned and looked at Bianca.

"Brat? Really, Bianca? I could turn around and drop you off, but one thing's for certain: I will see my godson. You either accept that little boy, who is very important to me, or you don't; however, I will not listen to you demean him!"

Bianca glared at him. "Is that just an excuse to see the mother, Maxwell? I saw the way you were looking at her at the christening you dragged me to. We should be working on how to get you elected. We don't…"

"First of all, Bianca, I haven't said that I was even going to run. Secondly, you are right; I care about Cayla. She is my friend, and I love that little boy. This is the last time I will say this. Either accept all parts of my life or find someone else you can control, because you will never control me. Let's clarify this relationship. I'm willing to allow you to accompany me around. I'll even go so far as to say I'm dating you, but it won't bother me to let you go." Max looked at the stunned expression on her face. "It's your call, babe."

"It will be good to see him again," she said through clenched teeth.

"It will, won't it," Max said and pulled off from the side of the road.

Bianca quietly fumed. She had a new mission. Get rid of that baby momma as soon as she could.

When Cayla heard the doorbell ring, she was sitting on the floor with Jonathan as he crawled around her, going for his favorite toy. She wasn't expecting anyone. She lifted the baby and went to answer the door. Seeing who had entered the house, Jonathan instantly reached for Max.

"Hey, Little Man," he greeted as he took the baby from his mother. "I hope you don't mind. I brought Bianca. We are on our way to my mother's house for dinner."

"Hi, come on in. Of course, I don't. Hello, Bianca," Cayla greeted politely.

Bianca moved past her without any acknowledgement and sat beside Max who had Jonathan on his knees. Cayla could only shake her head. This woman had serious issues. For Max, she would be polite if it killed her, but she was getting tired of everyone thinking she was a doormat that they could just wipe their dirty shoes on whenever they wanted. They were going to make her catch a case in a minute.

She closed the door. "May I offer you refreshments?" she smiled.

"Nothing for me," Max replied.

"I could use a glass of wine," Bianca said.

"Of course. Come in the kitchen, and I will fix it right up." The two ladies left Max to his playing with the baby. Bianca followed her out of the room.

"Please have a seat," Cay invited. "I have white and red."

"Red would be great," Bianca said as she sat at the breakfast bar.

Cayla poured her a glass and set it in front of her. She didn't know what to say to Bianca. She had come to terms with her being Max's lady. She leaned against the bar.

"So, Cayla, what do you do when you are not taking care of the baby?" Bianca asked before she sipped her wine.

"Before Jon's death, I was going to school for interior design. I was almost done. I had intended to start a business after I graduated."

"Wow, why don't you?" Bianca asked. *Perfect. This could be her chance to get rid of this albatross.*

Cayla shrugged. "I've been thinking about it, but I'm not sure now is the right time. My research tells me it takes a lot of time to startup a business; just cultivating relationships and making a positive name for myself takes a 110%. I don't want to take that amount of time away from my son right now, especially with his father not being here. I wouldn't mind working for someone else, but usually those positions are hard to come by."

"Are you any good at it?"

Cay smiled. "I think I am."

"Did you do this house?" Bianca asked, looking around.

"Yes, I did."

"It's nice." *Umph, what I want to say is I wouldn't let Cayla touch my house with a ten-foot pole,* Bianca silently thought.

"You think so?" Cayla asked excitedly.

"Yeah, really," Bianca lied. "Look, I have a friend that has his own interior design business. He may be in the market for a new designer. Do you have a portfolio?"

"Really?" She now was really getting excited.

"Hey, I tell you what; I'll talk to him. May I see your portfolio?"

"Yes, I'll be right back." Cay rushed out of the room.

"Hey, Cay, what's going on?"

"One minute, Max. I'm going to show Bianca my portfolio. She said she has a friend that may be looking for an interior designer."

Cayla returned with her portfolio. Max was in the kitchen, and he and Bianca were talking softly.

Cay placed the booklet on the bar. Bianca smiled at her and opened the book. Cay watched her as she turned page after page.

Max looked at Cayla. He could see the excitement in her eyes as Bianca studied the drawings and floorplans.

"These are really good," Bianca commented before she closed the portfolio.

"You truly think so?"

"Yes, my friend is always looking for someone with fresh ideas. Of course, it's the clients you have to please."

Max frowned. He wondered why Bianca was helping Cay. Bianca was not a generous person, unless there was something in it for her. Max moved around the counter and handed the baby to Cay.

"We have to go," he announced.

"Give me your number, and I promise I'll talk to him and get back to you," Bianca said as she rose from the stool.

"Wow, thanks, Bianca. I look forward to it."

"What was that all about?" Max asked suspiciously.

"What?" Bianca asked innocently.

"*I'll talk to my friend.* What friend?"

Bianca sighed. "I do have a friend that has his own design firm and is looking for a designer. Is that so hard to believe?"

"I got that. What I want to know is why are you helping Cayla?"

To get rid of her, she thought to herself.

"I asked her what she did before the baby. She said interior design and that she wouldn't mind working for someone else."

Max cut his eyes at her. "So you, out of the kindness of your heart, decided to help her. So again I say, why?"

"You're hurting my feelings. I'm not totally heartless. I'm trying here, Max. I see you are very fond of Cayla and the baby, and I just want you to know that I support you. When you decide to run for mayor, I'm sure they will be an important part of that."

Max reached over and took her hand.

"Thank you, baby."

Bianca smiled, thinking *if only he knew the real deal.*

*****

Friday, a week later, Cayla was sitting in the office of Dorsett Interior Design, one of the best firms in Atlanta. She of course had heard of them when she was in school. Some of the designers in the firm had even come in to teach a class or two when she was still attending the Institute of Design. Now here she sat nervously, with her portfolio clutched in her hand. True to her word, Bianca had set her up with an appointment. After she and Max had left her house that day, Cayla didn't expect much. She felt the bad vibes that rolled in waves off of Bianca. Even at the christening, she got the distinct feeling that Bianca wanted no part of Max's family, let alone her. So why suddenly did she want to help her? She was equally stunned when the call came that she had an appointment with Grant Dorsett, the owner of the firm. So here she sat, waiting to be seen by the man himself. Ms. Harriett agreed to watch Jonathan, so she didn't have to rush home. She was also encouraging her to finish up her degree.

"Ms. Sherman, Mr. Dorsett will see you now," the assistant said.

Cayla rose, smoothed down the skirt to her business suit and followed the assistant to Mr. Dorsett's office. She took a deep breath when the door was opened.

She then stepped inside the office. The assistant smiled and closed the door behind her.

Wow, Cayla thought. Behind the desk sat a very handsome blonde, blue-eyed man talking on the phone. She stood with her case in her hand, waiting until he acknowledged her presence.

He hung up the phone and then looked at her. His eyes trailed from her face to her feet before he rose and moved to the front of his desk.

"Cayla Sherman, I'm going to assume," he said in a rich deep tone.

"Yes," Cayla said as she extended her hand. His strong hand closed around hers a little tighter than she liked, but a strong handshake was a good thing, right?

"Please, Cayla, have a seat," he invited. "May I call you Cayla?" he asked with a sly grin on his face.

"Yes, of course," she said as she took the offered seat while he returned behind his desk. "So, you want to work for me?" Mr. Dorsett asked.

"Well, Mr. Dorsett, I would appreciate the opportunity, if you are willing to take a chance on me. I love designing and have attended design school. I have only a couple of classes remaining before I walk across the stage with my degree. However, due to tragic circumstances, I had to put school and my career on hold."

"Yes, Bianca told me you are a new widow and have a young son. I'm sorry for your loss."

"Thank you."

"Well, let's get down to business. Let me see your portfolio. Bianca says your specs look good."

"Yes, sir." Cayla handed him her book of designs and her resume.

Cay watched as he looked through her tablet. A few times he nodded his head. Finally, he closed it.

"Not bad, Cayla," he said. "I can offer you an entry level position. That means you assist the designers on staff, then gradually with their recommendations, I will see how you do with a client. Now I'm not promising you a permanent spot. This will be on a trial basis, just to see what you can handle and how well our clients work with you. We have some of the wealthiest clients in Atlanta, and my reputation is spotless."

Inwardly Cayla grinned.

"So, that being said, what do you say? Are you up for the challenge?"

Cayla smiled. "Yes, I'm willing to start at entry level."

"Great." Grant rose and extended his hand. "I'll see you on Monday."

"Thank you, Mr. Dorsett." Cayla grabbed her portfolio and left his office with lighter steps and hopes of fulfilling her long-time dreams. God is good….

Grant dialed Bianca, put her on speaker, and waited for her to answer. "Now what do you expect me to do with her?"

"Keep her busy. I want her out of the way, Grant," Bianca said.

Grant laughed. "Why did I know that you needed her out of the way? Is she in the way of you and your new man?"

"That new man is going to be the new mayor of Atlanta, and he is too fond of her and that brat of hers. I need Maxwell to focus on me and making me the First Lady of Atlanta. So be a dear and keep her out of my way."

"For you, darling, anything. You know that. Now what can I expect from you?"

Bianca chuckled. "What do you want?" she purred.

"Do I have to say it?" Grant chuckled.

"I'll see you tonight. And Dorsett?" she purred.

"Yes, Darlin'."

"Bring your A-game." Bianca ended the call.

Chapter Ten

Maxwell sat in his study swirling a snifter of cognac. He brought it to his lips and sipped the fine liquor. He couldn't believe he was contemplating running for mayor of the largest city in Georgia. He was a closet politician, and he had his opinions on how some areas in the city could be better run. He serves on the Board of Directors for the Council of State Chambers as Secretary-Treasurer and sits on the board of the Georgia Association of Chamber of Commerce Executives. Max serves on committees of HBCUs (Historical Black Colleges and Universities). Amazingly, he is also a member of the U.S. Chamber of Commerce's Council of 100, the U.S. Chamber's Board, and the Political Affairs Committee. He was named one of Georgia's 100 Most Influential Georgians and one of the Atlanta Business Chronicle's Most Influential Atlanteans. His platform was building communities, creating a productive educational structure that would work in the new millennium, and creating jobs and skill training facilities.

"What do you think, Jon? Could I run this town?" he asked in the empty room. Max chuckled. He knew his best friend would have been at his side encouraging him. Jon always said Max missed his calling in politics. He was a born leader; he knew that much about himself. When he had finally talked to his mother about what he was contemplating, she was behind him 100%. He drank the cognac. Yes, he was going to run for mayor. He lifted the phone and called the man who started this political bug to come alive in him. Also, there was one other person in particular he wanted to share his news with before he went public. He had to fix that tomorrow.

Cayla was leaning over the blueprint of her first project. She was designing the living room of a newly married couple with the means to have a designer. They lived in a gated Riverfront community. She had been with Dorsett Interior Design for two months. She had been with a few of the designers, and she knew that she had impressed them with her ideas. She was shocked when Mr. Dorsett called her into his office and told her how he had heard great things about her from his designers and was impressed with her work as well. He offered her the project, and she jumped on it. She had already met with the couple to get a feel of their likes and dislikes. Of course, she had to show her designs to the head designer for approval, but it wasn't the head designer she wanted to impress; it was the young couple. If they liked it, they would have her do the entire four-bedroom house. She already had three drawings for them, which she would be showing tomorrow. Cayla straightened and looked down at her work then smiled. She was ready for the presentation tomorrow. She gently rolled the drafts and banded them before putting them in the designer leather bag Max had given her as a gift when she took the job. She turned off the light over her drafting table and looked at her watch. It was three in the afternoon and time for Jonathan to wake up from his nap, if she wanted him to sleep tonight.

    She went to the nursery. He was standing up, holding on to the crib, and giving her a grin which showed his two bottom teeth. Cayla smiled. "Hey, sweet pea," she cooed, going to lift him out of the crib.

    "Somebody smells," she said, raining kisses over his face. She quickly changed him and put him into a onesie then took him to have a snack. At eight months, her son was already wearing clothes large enough for an eleven-month old. She predicted that he was going to be a big boy. His father was a tall man and nicely built.

    Cayla carried him out of the room just as her doorbell rang. "Who could that be, Jon?" she asked the cooing baby as she went to open the door.

    "Look who's here," Cayla said as she stepped aside to let him enter.

"Hey, Cay," Max greeted. "Hey, Little Man," he said. Jon's smile was now a grin as he reached for Maxwell.

"I'm just about to give him a snack," Cayla said and headed for the kitchen.

As always, her heart went crazy when she saw Max. It had been a couple of months since she'd seen him. When she'd started working again, he would visit the baby at his mother's, who watched him while Cayla worked.

Max was having the same thoughts. Now that she was working, they hadn't seen each other, and damn if he didn't miss her every single day.

"How you been, Cay?" Max asked as he followed her to the kitchen. He sat at the table and held Jon on his lap.

"I'm good. What about you?" she asked as she pulled out the snacks for the baby.

"I'm good. I went to Mom's. She said you were working from home today."

"Yeah," she said and carried over a baby dish with bananas. "You can feed him," she smiled.

Max lifted the spoon and put some in the baby's mouth. "What brings you here?" Cay asked as she sat across from him. Jon gave an impatient wail.

"You have to feed him faster than that, Max," she chuckled.

"Greedy kid," Max laughed.

He looked at her in between feeding the baby. He didn't answer her question. Instead he asked, "How's the job?"

"I love it. I got my first project," she replied proudly.

"Wow, that's great. I knew you'd be great, Cay," Max complimented.

"Thanks, Max. Now tell me why you are really here."

Because I miss you, he thought to himself. "I have been asked to run for Mayor of Atlanta," he said.

"Wow. Really? Are you going to?" Cay asked.

"I think I am. No... I am. I just wanted you to be the first to know, other than Mom, before I went public," he commented.

"Me? Really?"

"Of course. You're my friend, right? Do you think I'm being overzealous?"

"Are you kidding? I think you will make a great mayor. You are a born leader, Max, and you have the credentials to win. People love and admire the man you are. I know Ms. Harriett said as much. She must be very proud."

Max smiled. "Yeah, you know Mom. In the next month, I'm going to go public. Avery Chambers, my campaign manager, is getting me started. I have always liked and respected him. He was the one that convinced me to run."

"He must regard you highly if he wants you to run then. Congratulations, I'm proud of you," she said.

Max's eyes met hers, and he had to pull himself back before his heart jumped from his chest. He focused on the baby. He lifted and burped him then wiped his mouth. Max stood with the baby in his hands, preparing to leave.

"Hey, why don't you stay for dinner? You can play with Jon while I cook."

"I'd like that," Max said and walked out of the kitchen, blowing on the baby's face and making Jon giggle.

Bianca was fuming. She had been calling Max for the past hour, and it kept going to his voice mail. She had called his office earlier, and his assistant told her he was off-site and wasn't going to return to the office until tomorrow. Rudely she hung up on the woman. His ass better not be over at Cayla's house. She even called his mother. She told Bianca that she had no idea where Maxwell was and probably wouldn't tell her if she knew. She then hung the phone up on Bianca. She called Grant Dorsett's firm and found out Cayla was working from home today. She got Cayla's phone number, as she had thrown it away some time ago. She dialed the number. She knew it had been months since he'd seen Cayla. Dorsett was keeping her busy as Bianca requested. She knew Max still saw the brat at his mother's house. He told her directly that he will see his godson often and whenever he liked. She hadn't sorted that problem out yet but she would, and then the ball would be in her court. She dialed the number.

Bianca put the phone on speaker.

Max sat Jon in the highchair and was feeding him dinner when Cayla's phone rang. She looked at the number and frowned. "Hello."

"Hi, Cayla, it's Bianca."

"Hi, Bianca, how are you?" she asked politely.

"Have you seen Max?" she asked rudely. Cayla looked over at Max.

He shook his head.

"I'm sorry; I haven't," she lied, narrowing her eyes at him and not pleased.

"Has he been there?" Bianca asked tightly.

"No, he hasn't. Did you try his phone?"

"Of course I did," she snapped. "Bye!"

Bianca left her condo, fuming. Cayla was lying through her teeth, Bianca thought, so she would have to do a little drive-by and see for herself.

Cay hung up the phone and sat at the table. "She was very rude," Cay commented.

"I'm not in the mood for Bianca tonight. I'll call her later," he said and focused on Jon.

Cay shook her head. "Why are you with her if you have to hide from her?"

Max shrugged. Inwardly he thought: *She is the buffer that keeps me from making you my woman.* "She can sometimes be overbearing."

"She sounds possessive to me," Cay said under her breath.

"What did you say?" Max asked, frowning.

Bianca drove past Cayla's house. When she saw Maxwell's car parked in the driveway, she parked a block from the house, screamed at the top of her lungs and banged on the steering wheel until her hands were sore. "That lying bitch," she hissed. She was not going to sit by idly and let that witch take her man and ruin her future of being the *First Lady of Atlanta*. She was going to get rid of that brat too. Maxwell's attention should be focused on her and winning the mayoral race. Cayla and that kid weren't going to know what hit them when she finished.

Avery Chambers looked at the young man with pride. He was thrilled Maxwell had decided to toss his hat in the ring of politics. He was a natural at it because he had been a gifted student while studying under Avery during his tenure as a professor of political science at prestigious Morehouse College. Although Maxwell's major was architectural engineering, he had also minored in political science. He was very impressed with the young man's mind, and he was a natural debater. Over the years, they had become very close friends. They would meet for dinner at least once a month and talk politics. During one of those dinners, the mayoral idea came up, and Avery had been trying diligently ever since to encourage Max to throw his hat in the ring. He was presently on several committees and what he had done in those committees was well noted. Avery wasn't the only person who thought he should run. Maxwell had politics down to a science, knowing the city's assets and liabilities. He didn't mind voicing his opinion regardless of whose toes he stepped on. Maxwell, in his view, was the perfect candidate for this city to thrive; he would do great things for its people. It also didn't hurt that he was handsome and had a swagger that turned the ladies' heads. He had a quiet strength about him, and he commanded the room the moment he entered it. Max was highly respected and loved by the residents of Atlanta. He was damned near perfect. Avery also had the pleasure of meeting Maxwell's widowed mother a few years back. His mother was a beautiful woman with a kind heart and a spunky persona that instantly captured his attention. He was instantly smitten. Avery just smiled. Maybe this would give him the opportunity to get to know her better. He was a young sixty-year-old and still had all his hair, with a little gray threaded throughout. He kept himself in excellent physical condition. He ran every day and went to the gym twice a week. And the women still considered him handsome. Yep, he should still be able to get his *Mack* on and enjoy Mrs. Harriett's company. He was quite the ladies' man. He dated when the need hit him but nothing serious. He was now retired and wealthy beyond his own needs. He laughed and then became somewhat somber with thoughts of his deceased wife of thirty years. It never crossed his mind to remarry or date exclusively. He and his wife were never blessed with children, but it didn't deter the love they had for one another. To love like that again would be a fantasy. Avery pushed his hand through his thick blonde/gray hair, trying to get back into the frame of mind to meet with Maxwell this morning. Yes, he was excited to get started with the planning of the campaign to make Maxwell the next and best mayor Atlanta had ever elected.

"Where were you last night?" Bianca irately demanded when Max answered his phone.

"Good morning to you too, Bianca," Max said sarcastically.

"Good morning. Now, where were you?" she repeated.

"I went to Cayla's to see my godson," he told her.

"I called and she said you were not there. When I see that little…"

"I told her to tell you that. Trust me, she was not happy about that, and if you see her, you better be polite," Max warned.

Bianca didn't say another word.

"I have a meeting with Avery Chambers this morning, so maybe we can meet for lunch afterwards. I may have some news that might make your day," Max said.

"Really? I look forward to seeing you. How about The Bistro at 1pm," Bianca said.

"Fine, I'll see you later." Max hung up the phone.

Bianca started dancing and singing around her house. She knew he was going to tell her he was going to run for mayor. She just knew! She raised her hands and shimmied some more. "I'm going to be Atlanta GA's First Lady, Bianca Steele-Washington," she repeatedly sang at the top of her lungs.

Suddenly, she lowered her arms. She was still going to get rid of Cayla and that little brat. Damn it, she thought. Grant Dorsett should have had Cayla distracted and under his thumb by now. But the asshole said he genuinely liked her and was very impressed with her designing skills. Now she just had to play down and dirty. She didn't have a plan yet but it would come, and when it did, it would be explosive.

Margaret Sherman left her lawyer's office, and she was not happy with the outcome. She had hired a custody lawyer to try to get her grandson away from *Ms. Ghetto Central.* She choked up when she remembered holding him at the christening. He was Jon's image when he was that age. She had to get her grandson by any means necessary, and then she would have her son back. However, the lawyer told her if she couldn't prove that the mother was unfit, there was nothing he could do for her. That was the third lawyer that told her the exact same thing. She was lucky the last two didn't charge her for the consultation. She had even gone to see Harriett Washington. She implored her to help her convince Cayla to let her see her grandson. Harriett said in no uncertain terms, *"With the way you have treated the girl? If I tell her anything, it would be to encourage her not to allow you to see him."*

She had always hated Harriett Washington, who acted as if Margaret put a bad taste in her mouth. She pulled the door open to the Lord and Taylor department store. What she needed was a little shopping therapy to take her mind off of things.

Bianca was browsing through the dresses in the Belle Badgley Mischka section in Lord and Taylor when she looked up and saw a familiar face walking toward her. The lady was elegantly dressed and carried herself with an air of haughtiness. She didn't forget a face, and she had seen that one somewhere. Bianca snapped her fingers. That's it. She was the grandmother to that brat of Cayla's. From what she observed and overheard from her and the two young women with her, they despised Cayla as well. They weren't introduced at the christening, so she didn't know her name.

Bianca stepped out into the aisle just as Margaret Sherman walked past her. "Hello," Bianca greeted.

Margaret stopped and looked at the young woman. "Yes?"

"I know we don't know one another but weren't you at the christening for Cayla Sherman's baby?" she asked politely.

Margaret frowned. "Yes, I was," she replied.

"I was also there. I'm dating Maxwell. He dragged me along because of his fondness for the baby," Bianca said with a roll of her eyes.

"Oh yes, I did see you with Maxwell. At least he's not with that gold digging Cayla," Margaret hissed.

Bianca leaned forward. "You don't like her either?" Bianca whispered craftily.

"No, that wench is the reason my son Jonathan is dead. She has stolen his estate, which was considerable, and now she has his son and refuses to let me see him," Margaret complained.

"I understand the feeling well. She's been trying to take Maxwell from me and is using that baby to do it. I'm at my wits' end as to what to do about it. Max loves the little boy so much." Bianca tried to look crestfallen.

"Why don't we have coffee someplace and talk about how we can stop that wench from taking my grandson and Maxwell. He was, after all, my son's best friend," Margaret offered.

"By the way, I'm Bianca Steele." She extended her hand, smiling.

Margaret smiled. "I'm Margaret Sherman."

Chapter Eleven

Maxwell followed Avery inside the building that would be their campaign headquarters. Avery stood back and let Max take it all in. "This place is huge," he commented, looking over at Avery.

"Just think, in a few weeks it will be buzzing with activity. Volunteers, fundraising committee, political strategists, lawyers, and anyone else we will need to get you elected."

"You were prepared for me to accept this challenge, huh?"

Avery grinned. "I was hopeful. You're a good man, son. I have always admired you, and you have made a name for yourself in the community. Plus, you are a political genius. You have absorbed everything I've taught you. I'm very proud of the man you have become, and you will be good for this city. This is the last term for the present mayor. I think you are a great replacement, and I know he will endorse you."

Maxwell felt heat creep up his neck. He was flattered by the praise. "I will be running against a tough opponent in Thomas Rashford," Maxwell said.

"Yeah, but this is the Dem's year. We both know that, right?"

Max nodded. "I'm ready to do this," he said confidently.

"Well, let's get started." Avery showed him the rest of the building. It had offices and a large open area where they would have TV appearances.

As he followed Avery around the rooms, he thought of the lunch he had with Bianca earlier. She had seemed to be in a good mood. When he told her he decided to run for mayor, she forgot all decorum and shouted loudly. She had been pestering him about running, but they had only known each other less than a year. Was her blind faith in him for real? He had never told her anything about his past, because it never came up. Everything was usually about her. Actually, there was not much on her past either, but she adored the spotlight. He hoped…

"So what do you think?" Avery asked, breaking into his thoughts.

"It's great," Maxwell commented. "I'm sure my mother will want to volunteer."

Avery smiled inwardly. "Of course. The mother of the next mayor is important to the campaign."

They left the building. "Why don't you come to my mother's for dinner? I know you've met, but that was years ago," Max said. "I'll give her a call."

"If it's no trouble...."

"You're my campaign manager. You have to get to know my family, and I want you to meet my godson and his mom, Cayla. They are an important part of my life as well."

Avery looked at him. "Aren't you dating someone exclusively?"

"Yes, Bianca Steele. She relocated here from Ohio. Her company has opened a branch in Atlanta," Max explained.

"You know we have to do a check on her and Cayla," Avery said.

"Yeah, I know. We don't want any surprises, because when I announce that I'm running, Rashford is going to do some checking of his own."

"That's what I'm talking about. Son, you got this. Call me with the dinner time." Avery shook his hand and made his way to his car.

Bianca was elated at the turn of events. She had met the one person that could help her get rid of Cayla. Discrediting people was her forte. After all, that was how she rose to the top as VP in one of America's oldest international companies. Actually, she was sent to Atlanta because she had threatened to expose the company for the many discrepancies she found in their record keeping, discrepancies she initiated. She chuckled. It would have taken her years to move up the corporate ladder if she played nice. Therefore, she stepped on a few heads, stabbed a few backs, had a few fired and even slept with many. *Next step, First Lady of Atlanta!* She giggled and sipped her wine. Life couldn't get any better. She was going to do everything in her power to get Maxwell elected. She was going to be on his arm at every rally, dinner, and debate. She was going to make herself known to the city of Atlanta. Next, he was going to propose. She would make sure that happened after Ms. Cayla was out of the equation.

Cayla arrived at Harriett's house to pick up Jonathan. When Cay walked in, Harriett was in a state of anxiousness. She was running around making sure the house was just right. She had on a housecoat and her hair was tied down with a silk scarf.

"The baby is still asleep. You need to go home and change. Maxwell is bringing over his campaign manager, and I want to make a good impression. So go change and be back here by seven o'clock," she ordered.

Cayla watched as Harriett rushed past her, back into the dining room, and placed her good china on the table.

"Ms. Harriett," Cay called, trying not to laugh. She had never seen her so flustered.

"Girl, get going. Jon's going to be fine. I'll dress him for dinner." She looked at her watch. "It's five o'clock. Get moving, child."

"Okay, I'll be back in time."

Cayla and Maxwell arrived at his mother's house at the same time. They looked at each other and smiled.

"Have you spoken to your mom today?" Cay asked.

"Every hour on the hour," Max admitted. "What's going on?"

"She wants to make a good impression on your campaign manager. She made me go home and change when I came to pick up Jonathan. I've never seen her so nervous," Cayla said.

Max frowned. "Nervous? Mom?"

"Wait until you see her," Cay said as she opened the door.

Harriett stopped when the door opened. "Hello, children. We have one hour before Mr. Chambers arrives. Maxwell, go up and shave away some of that shadow off your face. Cay, I left Jon's change of clothes on the couch; dress him, please. I didn't get a chance. I'm going to check on dinner." She left the room. Max and Cay looked at each other.

When Harriett returned, they still hadn't moved. She stopped and clapped her hands. "CHOP! CHOP!"

Fifteen minutes before the guest arrived, they were sitting in the living room. Max was in awe of his beautiful mother. His mother looked more beautiful than he had seen her in a long time. She had on a belted floral dress that showed that his mother still had it going on. Her usually long hair was pulled back tonight, and it looked sleek in the bun at the back of her head. She had that classy, rich woman look, and she wore it well. Even baby Jonathan was dressed in a cute little suit. Harriett was holding Jon and told him he better be on his best behavior, and the baby giggled up at her.

Cay and Max couldn't get over his mother. "She's very proud of you, Max," Cayla whispered. "She just wants you to look good to your manager."

"Avery is a great man. He's really going to be impressed."

The doorbell rang and Harriett stood. She handed the baby off to Cay. "Max, please answer the door and bring Mr. Chambers into the sitting room," she instructed. She smoothed her hand over her hair, smoothed down the skirt of her dress and put a smile on her face.

"Ms. Harriett, is this your first time meeting him?" Cay asked.

"I met him years ago, not long after my husband passed. He was very supportive of Max even back then, and they have remained friends over the years. If I remember, Mr. Chamber was a very handsome man. He has very interesting blue eyes."

Cay's eyebrows rose and then dipped.

They could hear the two men talking in the foyer before they came into the sitting room.

Cay looked at Mr. Chambers. For an older man, he was quite good looking - and wearing the hell out of that Armani suit. Max led him over to his mother. "Avery, this is Harriett Washington, my mom," Max introduced.

"Mrs. Washington, it's a pleasure to see you again. You are as lovely as I remember," Avery said, taking Harriett's hand.

"Thank you, Mr. Chambers. Welcome to my home," Harriett said, enjoying his hand. Max could swear his mother's cheeks reddened.

Max turned to Cay, who was now standing with Jonathan in her arms. "Avery, this is Cayla Sherman and Jonathan. You remember my old friend Jonathan, whom we lost in a tragic accident. This is his widow and son."

"It's nice to meet you, Mr. Chambers," Cay said as Max took Jonathan from her arms.

Avery took her hand in his. "I'm sorry for your loss, Mrs. Sherman. Jon was a good man. I know how close he and Max were. He is truly missed." He turned to the baby. "Yes, I see Jon all over him. He has you, and that is a good thing. Right, little fellow?" He even shook the little hand of Jonathan, who simply stared at the stranger.

"Please, Mr. Chambers, have a seat," Harriett invited. She sat on the sofa, and he sat beside her.

Max and Cay sat across from them, with Max holding the baby.

"Mr. Chambers…"

"Please call me Avery," he coaxed.

"Okay, Avery, and you may call me Harriett. I'm not a woman who minces words. I'm very proud of my son, but do you really think he has a chance at winning this election?"

"I wouldn't have asked if I didn't think he did." Avery went on to praise Max's accomplishments and all he has done for the city, some of which had gone unnoticed because of Max's modesty. When he finished, Max was grinning, and Cay and Harriett were beaming proudly.

"Shall we have dinner, Mr. Chambers? It's a simple fare: roast beef, roasted potatoes and carrots."

Avery lifted his elbow to Harriett, and she took it as they walked away.

Cayla and Maxwell glanced at each other. "I think Mr. Chambers is smitten," Cay giggled.

Max smiled. "It would appear so."

"I haven't tasted a meal like that in many years," Avery said, wiping his mouth. "My compliments to the chef."

"Oh, go on with you," Harriett giggled. "You are welcome to dinner anytime, Avery. And since you and my son will be working closely together, I will probably be seeing more of you, right?"

Avery's smiled widened. "I guess you're right. Maybe you would consider helping out at the office?"

"Anything you need," Harriett returned his smile.

Cay and Max watched the older couple and smiled. Max cleared his throat.

"I'm going to take the baby to the nursery," Cay said, retrieving him from Maxwell's arms and rising with the sleeping baby in her arms.

"Need help?" Max offered.

"No, I got him," she smiled.

"Coffee and dessert in the sitting room," Harriett called as she also rose. "You like peach cobbler, Avery?" she asked.

"Love it," he said. "Can I help with something?"

"No, no, make yourself comfortable. I won't be long."

Cay returned, and they had a lovely conversation. Max even asked if Cay could come and make his office efficient, since he would be using it for at least a year before the election. Cay quickly agreed. Avery made a date for Harriett and Cayla to see the new headquarters this weekend.

They ate cobbler and talked for a while. Before long, it was past eleven. They said their goodnights, and Avery said he looked forward to seeing the ladies this weekend.

Bianca looked at her phone. She had been waiting for Maxwell to call her. She thought that they would go out tonight to celebrate his running for mayor, but he had a dinner meeting with his campaign manager, whom she had yet to meet. He didn't even tell her where they were dining. If she had known, she would have happened upon them and introduced herself to them. It was past eleven, and he still hadn't called. She couldn't wait any longer. She pressed the number that connected her to him. It went to voicemail. She sighed, annoyed. *"Be patient, Bianca. The pot of gold is just within your grasp. Be patient, girl."*

One thing for sure she was going to stress the importance of Maxwell taking her calls at all times.

Harriett and Cayla, with baby Jonathan in her arms, followed as Avery gave them the tour of the campaign headquarters. Cayla mentally thought of what she could do to make the space efficient yet comfortable. The tour ended at the large ballroom. Avery explained the room would host a lot of activities. The first would be a press conference after announcing Maxwell's running for the office of mayor.

"It's a nice building, Avery," Harriett said, smiling up at him.

Wow, Avery thought. "Yes, ma'am. Now tell me, could I offer you the job of sitting your pretty self behind a desk to check those that come through the front door?"

Harriett smiled. "I will help in any capacity you need me."

Cayla turned away. *Was Ms. Harriett flirting?*

"Wonderful," he said, grinning. As they went back down the short flight of stairs to the first floor, the door opened, and Maxwell entered with Bianca beside him.

Bianca stopped, surprised. When Max picked her up, she insisted he show her where the headquarters were going to be. She didn't expect they would not be alone.

"What are they doing here?" she hissed to Max.

Max frowned at her. "Why wouldn't they be here?" he asked and walked away to greet Cayla and his mother. He reached for the baby, who gladly went into his arms.

Harriett's eyes were on Bianca as she glared at Max's back before her face righted itself.

"Mrs. Washington, so good to see you again. Hello, Cayla," she smiled a smile that did not reach her sneaky eyes.

"Hi, Bianca, how are you?" Cayla said, smiling at her.

"Bianca," Harriett muttered.

Bianca's eyes shifted to Avery Chambers. "And you are?" she said as he moved closer to the group.

Avery's eyes narrowed quickly. He smiled mildly. "I am Avery Chambers, campaign manager, and who might you be?" She was a bit thrown. Maxwell hadn't mentioned her to his campaign manager? Why?

Bianca extended her hand and glanced at Max who was occupied with the baby. "If Maxwell could take a minute, he would introduce me." All eyes shifted to Max who was enjoying his godson. "I'm Bianca Steele, a very close friend of Maxwell's."

Avery took her hand as she smiled at him. Bianca wondered if she could get him on her side of this campaign. He could be useful.

"Maxwell," she called kind of snappishly.

"Yes," he turned his head and looked at Bianca. "Really, Maxwell," she said impatiently.

"Sorry, but this little guy distracted me," he said as he lifted him above his head as Jonathan giggled.

Harriett looked at Bianca. "He really loves that little boy," she commented.

Bianca looked at Cayla, who purposely remained silent. Maxwell joined the group.

"I'm going to assume you know of Maxwell's bid for Mayor of Atlanta?" Bianca said.

"Of course," Harriett said. "I'm so very proud of him." She looked fondly at her son.

Cay smiled at Max, who smiled back at her. "Did Cay tell you she agreed to decorate the office to make it efficient and Zen-like," Max boasted.

Cay shook her head. "Efficient, I can do," she said, grinning at Max.

Bianca looked at her. "Does Dorsett know you are moonlighting? I thought his staff couldn't work outside the firm without asking him," Bianca said spitefully.

"Well, I have spoken to Mr. Dorsett, and I told him this is on a voluntary basis. He was very supportive." Cay's eyes met Bianca's.

Inwardly, Bianca was fuming.

"When can you start?" Max asked, smiling.

"We can go over what you want and then go from there," Cay offered.

"Great, let's go look at the office I've chosen for myself," Max said. Cay followed him as they walked away with the baby still in his arms.

"So, Ms. Steele, how do you feel about Maxwell's running for office?" Avery asked.

"I think it's wonderful. I would like to help with his campaign. I have a few good strategic ideas I think will get Maxwell elected."

Avery's eyebrows dipped. "So you've worked on a campaign before?" he asked.

"Well no, but I am acquainted with a few politicians that could help him. I think my best help will be on his fundraising campaign and public relations. I know several wealthy people who would donate to his campaign." She smiled. "I would like to talk in-depth with you, Mr. Chambers," she said coquettishly.

She looked at Harriett. "I guess you will be handing out flyers and such, Mrs. Washington," Bianca said with a tilt of her lips.

"Oh no, my dear. I will be in the thick of things. I will be his office manager," Harriett smiled and glanced over at Avery. Bianca glanced between Avery and Harriett.

"Well, I'm pleased to say that Mrs. Washington will be perfect in that capacity. I will speak with you further about fundraising, Ms. Steele, as you say that is your forte," Avery said. "As far as public relations goes, I have already hired the best PR firm in Atlanta. I have worked with them before, and they are the best in the business."

Bianca's eyes narrowed on Avery, then on Harriett. *Harriett's going to be a problem,* she thought. *I will have to rectify that little problem and show them who's in charge - below the radar of course.*

Chapter Twelve

Avery wasn't pleased when word was leaked out to the news media about Maxwell's bid for mayor. Neither Max nor Avery wanted to speculate about the leak. Officially, the announcement would be made tonight at the black tie meet-and-greet. Avery moved around the ballroom of the Intercontinental Buckhead Hotel, with Harriett on his arm. He glanced over at her. She looked absolutely stunning tonight. They had arrived early so Avery could make sure everything was in place. Broderick Matthews, the PR rep, joined them. Avery greeted him with a shake of his hand. Broderick had invited the Who's Who of Atlanta, and all of them had RSVP'd.

Broderick was new with the PR firm. He was young but had already made a name for himself with the firm. Avery had heard wonderful things about him.

"Mr. Chambers," he greeted, shaking his hand. "Mrs. Washington, you are stunning."

"Boy, please, but thank you," Harriett smiled.

"The guests should be arriving in a couple of hours, and everything is in place," Broderick said. I have arranged a small fifteen-minute press conference in the side room after the meet-and-greet for Mr. Washington. There, he can answer questions, which I have supplied to the press - at least for his first conference. I would like to get a picture of his family. After the announcement is made official tonight, the news hounds will be out in droves, so we must be careful what we expose to the press from this point on. Let's not forget, his opponent will be looking for any and everything on Mr. Washington, his family, and close associates."

"Yes, I know how this works, Broderick," Avery said. He glanced at Harriett. "You ready for this?"

"Hey, I can handle it."

Broderick cleared his throat. They looked at him. "Who is Ms. Bianca Steele to Mr. Washington?" he asked.

Harriett rolled her eyes. Avery had a feeling she wasn't too fond of Bianca. His first impression of Bianca was a woman who's very ambitious and strong with a touch of manipulation mixed in. She had made her way to his office after their first meeting at the headquarters. It was a conversation he wouldn't be forgetting anytime soon.

"Mr. Chambers, if you think to exclude me out of the campaign, you'd better think again. I will be Maxwell's wife. Let's get that straight here and now so that there will be no misunderstanding later on down the road," she had said after all the pleasantries were done.

"Excuse me. I didn't think Maxwell had plans to marry any time soon," Avery said.

"Well, not yet, but we have spoken of it. So I want to be by his side at all times when he's out in public."

"Well, I tell you what. Why don't you, Max and I talk about this over dinner?"

Bianca stood. *"That is all I'm asking, and we can meet anytime and anywhere."* She left his office.

Avery pushed the thought away. "Has she spoken to you?" Avery asked Broderick.

"Yes, sir. She wanted me to make implications to the press that she and Maxwell are engaged."

Avery was instantly pissed. "You will do no such thing until we have spoken to Maxwell, understood? You don't take any orders or directions from Ms. Steele. They are dating and that is all. It will be made public only if Maxwell wants that known."

Broderick smiled. "Yes, sir."

Harriett looked up at Avery. "I think she is going to be a problem," she stated.

"Don't worry. I will take care of Ms. Steele. She has met her match. I will let her know that she's not running anything."

"Bianca, come on before I leave you," Max snapped. "You were supposed to be ready over an hour ago. The meet-and-greet starts in forty-five minutes, and we still have to stop by and pick up Cayla."

Bianca came out of the room, still in her robe. "I'm hurrying. I had a meeting that ran late," she lied.

Max rolled his eyes. "Come on, Bianca. Get a move on."

Bianca turned and left him, with a wide smile on her face. She made sure that Cayla wouldn't be attending this function. It pissed her off that Max was having her arrive with them. This was Bianca's spotlight - *her time to shine.*

Max pulled out his phone and called Cayla.

"Cay, I'm sorry. I'm running late and won't have time to come and pick you up."

"Max, it's okay. You just get there. I can come to the next one," Cay said.

Max was feeling bad. "You sure, honey?"

"Hey, this is about you, not me. I can watch it on the news when you make your announcement. Have a good time, and good luck."

"Let's go, Bianca!" he shouted.

Bianca gave herself another look in the full-length mirror. She looked beautiful in the asymmetric satin-crepe Jason Wu gown that bared just a little of her back. Her hair, she flat-ironed and let hang around her shoulders with just a hint of curl. Smiling, she was pleased with her appearance. She blew herself a kiss in the mirror. "Girl, you look like a million bucks." She went and joined Max.

"Let's go," he said impatiently.

Bianca looked at the diamond watch on her wrist. "Honey, I don't think we will have time to pick up Cayla," she said innocently. "I'm sorry about this."

"I've already spoken to Cayla. She told us to go on without her." He walked away from Bianca.

"Oh, Max, I'm sorry." Max missed the look of joy and triumph in her eyes. *Oh, yes, this is only the beginning, little girl. You just wait. The best is yet to come.*

When Maxwell and Bianca entered the room, she made sure to be glued to his side. He looked for Avery and his mother. He had made it just in the nick of time.

"You were cutting it close," Avery replied. Harriett looked behind her son and instantly knew the reason why from the smirk on his companion's face.

"Where's Cayla?" Harriett asked.

Max cut his eyes at Bianca. "I was running late, so she told me to go on ahead." That was all he got out, as Broderick came to get him and take him away from the group.

Harriett looked at Bianca. "You wouldn't happen to know why Cayla couldn't make it, now would you?"

"All Max said was he wasn't dressed yet and she told him to go on." She shrugged. "I think it was thoughtful of her not to make him late. I see some friends, so if you will excuse me...."

"That wench is lying," Harriett hissed.

Avery patted her hand. "Don't get yourself worked up, Harriett. Let's go to our table."

Maxwell got a standing ovation when he officially announced he would be running for office. His speech was uplifting and motivating. Harriett and Avery smiled proudly. Bianca sat at another table, pouting. She should have been sitting at his table. She even confronted Max's PR man and asked him why she wasn't sitting at the head table. Broderick saw Bianca for what she was: a manipulator.

"I'm sorry, Ms. Steele, but it is important that those who can help with the campaign have that honor, and of course his family. Unless Mr. Washington specifically wants you at the table, then...." he explained.

"But there is an empty seat," she said.

"Yes, unfortunately Mrs. Cayla Sherman couldn't make it, and it was too late to make the changes. Have a wonderful evening." Broderick hurried away from Bianca.

Later as the people mingled and talked, Max excused himself and followed Broderick into a side room. Bianca followed but was stopped. "I should be with Maxwell," she complained.

"This is for the candidate only," Broderick told her and closed the door in her face.

Bianca's eyes narrowed. She had to get rid of that asshole too.

When the party ended, Max slipped into the limo. He couldn't help thinking that Cayla should have been there. For the rest of the evening, Bianca continued pouting like a spoiled child.

"I can't believe you introduced me as a good friend, Max. We are more than just good friends," she said once they were seated in the limo.

Max cut his eyes at her. "And I'm still pissed that you almost had me late for my first function. If you can't be on time, then I will not be escorting you," he snapped in irritation and looked out the window.

"I'm sorry, Max. It couldn't be helped."

"Next time - if there is one - I will just leave you."

This evening was not going well for her. Maybe she should step back just a bit. *No, not likely.* "You should have introduced me as your girlfriend, Max," she pouted and slid closer to him. She put her head on his shoulder and slid her hand under his jacket, rubbing his chest.

Max pulled her hand away from him, dropped it in her lap and glared at her.

Bianca gasped. "I'm sorry, Max. It won't happen again."

"I know." He turned away. The driver stopped outside her home.

"You coming up?" she asked.

"No! Goodnight, Bianca."

"Are you serious, Max?"

"As a heart attack, Bianca. There will be no celebrating with you until you can get yourself together and realize that this is a momentous time in my life." He dismissed her and turned back to look out of the window.

The driver opened the door for a stunned Bianca, who couldn't believe what Max had just done.

Maxwell slid onto the family pew beside Cayla, Nonna and his mother. Cay smiled, and Jonathan let out a squeal and reached for him. Cayla smiled up at him. Nonna and Harriett smiled over at him before they looked at the pastor speaking the word. Cayla leaned in to the baby and sniffed.

"He did a doodle," she whispered to Max. Cay reached down for the diaper bag.

"I'll take care of him," Max said and took the bag before slipping from the pew with Jonathan in his arms.

Margaret Sherman watched as Maxwell left the sanctuary with her grandson. She slipped out of the pew and followed.

Max laid the baby on the layette in the nursery. When Mrs. Sherman walked in, Max had removed Jonathan's clothes and was wiping his little bottom.

"Woo-hoo, boy, you need to be on the toilet," he said and laughed when the baby giggled up at him.

Margaret cleared her throat, startling Max. Max turned. This was all he needed.

"Good morning, Mrs. Sherman," he said.

"May I see him?" she asked.

"Sure, Mrs. Sherman." After he had cleaned him up, Max lifted the baby.

If he didn't know Mrs. Sherman so well, he would feel sorry for her. She looked at the baby with tears glistening in her eyes.

"He looks so much like Jon," she said softly. "Hi, little Jonathan, I'm your grandma," she said and lifted her hands to him.

Jonathan frowned at her before he pulled away and laid his head on Max's shoulder. Margaret reached up and took the baby from his arms. Instantly, Jonathan started to cry and reached for Max.

Max took him from her. Her eyes narrowed on him as he quieted the baby.

"He's not used to strangers," Max said.

"I'm not a stranger. I'm his grandmother," she snapped. "I don't appreciate that woman keeping him out of our lives. She has taken everything from me, and now she is turning my grandson against me. I won't have it. I won't stop until I have full custody of him," she threatened.

Oh, there she is, Max thought. He was waiting for the real Mrs. Sherman to make an appearance. "No court in the land will give custody of this baby to you. Cayla is a good mother. If…"

"When I reveal her true character, no judge will let her keep him. And if you were smart, you wouldn't associate yourself with her, especially with you running for mayor. She is going to dirty up your chance to win with her in your life. You just wait and see, Maxwell. You will regret even knowing Cayla." Mrs. Sherman turned and walked out of the nursery.

Max shook his head. This was all he needed: Hurricane Sherman.

Margaret didn't return to the sanctuary. She left the church and called her new best friend. "Can we meet for lunch?" Margaret said into the phone. "Good, see you in thirty minutes at The Bistro.

Margaret lifted her hand when she saw Bianca enter the restaurant. Bianca joined her at the corner table. After sitting, Margaret told her about what happened in church. Of course she had her embellishments. Bianca in turn told her about the meet-and-greet and how disappointed she had been. However, she was thrilled to tell her what she did to keep Cayla from the affair.

"I don't want to hurt Maxwell's chances of becoming mayor, but I will if they keep my grandson away from me," she stated.

Now, she couldn't have that and mess up her chance at being first lady. "What do you have on Cayla?" Bianca asked. After meeting Margaret Sherman, she had done her own little investigation on the self-righteous Mrs. Margaret Sherman. Margaret better do her right, for she had a lot of bones pushing at her closet door. Bianca inwardly smiled. *It's always good to have an ace up your sleeve.*

"Just that she was born on the wrong side of the tracks. I still think she tricked my son into marrying her. She was probably on drugs or something or selling her body to those people she hung out with," Margaret huffed.

Bianca tapped her chin. "I think I can arrange that. Come up with some pictures from her early years. I have friends that can make an angel look like the devil himself. Where is she from?"

"She's from one of the toughest areas of Atlanta."

Parents; what about her parents?"

"She was raised in foster care."

"Good, we can come up with a story of her upbringing and where she was from. I'll go to this place and see if I can find her old friends then buy me a story." Bianca grinned.

Margaret looked at her, frowning. "That's going to help you get her away from Maxwell, but how is that going to help me get my grandson?" Margaret asked.

"Oh, we are going to give CPS (Child Protection Services) a call. We will anonymously report that we saw her beating the kid in public. Then if we have to, we will release the phony video to Facebook. You won't believe the responses we'll get about it. By the time they figure it all out, you will have your grandson."

Margaret grinned. "What about Maxwell?"

When I finish reporting this story, he will have no choice but to distant himself from Cayla. If his PR rep is good, he will make sure that Max stays away from Cayla." *Then I will ride in on my white horse….*

Bianca and Margaret grinned at each other. "When do we start?" Margaret said.

"It has to happen gradually. We don't want to rush this and make mistakes in our haste. I'll take care of everything once I receive the pictures from you. Remember, we must not show our hand. Agreed?"

Chapter Thirteen

Within three months, the news of Maxwell Washington running for mayor caught fire. He now had more volunteers than he ever imaged. He had the support, of course, of his Phi Beta Sigma brothers who were equally proud and offered assistance as well. He had kids from several different area school districts making posters and flyers and disbursing them throughout the city. Maxwell was knee-deep into his campaign and had hit the floor running. He wanted to include the communities in his campaign, for he was fighting for a better life for both them and future little Atlanteans. The Democratic Headquarters' phones were ringing off the hook with people offering praise and help to get the voters to come out. They also set into motion a proposal for van transportation to the polls for the disabled, elderly or voters without transportation. Max even went door to door with the volunteers when he had free time.

Max was at his desk looking at the latest polls. So far in this short time, he was twenty percent ahead of Rashford. However, it wasn't enough; they still had months before the election. He was fully out of his architect business, but he had reliable people that worked for him who would keep the torch burning. His second-in-command had it all handled. That was one less worry. His phone buzzed, and he looked at the screen. He shook his head before putting it on speaker.

"Hello, Bianca," he spoke.

"Max, when are we going to spend time together?" she complained.

"Didn't we just have dinner two days ago? You know I'm busy. The rally is next week, and I'm sure you are not going to miss that. I have to be prepared and on top of things, Bianca."

"If you would let me have more responsibility than just answering phones and stuffing envelopes, we would see more of each other."

Max rolled his eyes. "Why is that so important, you being seen with me?" he asked impatiently.

"I'm your girlfriend, and I think it's time you announced me as such - or do you view me as just a side piece?" she snapped.

"Not doing that, Bianca, and I would never demean you in such a manner. I respect all women as jewels, so trust that I'm always thinking of you."

There was a brief pause from her and then a sigh. "Well alright then. But Max, I can handle the press. I could even help with your agenda."

"No, that is Avery and Broderick's jobs, and I will not incorporate you into the mix unless they ask for assistance."

"Let me warn you about Avery," she hissed. "I don't think he is to be trusted."

"Well, *I* trust him. I've known him a lot longer than I've known you. We have had this discussion before, Bianca, and the result remains the same." He exhaled. "Look, I've got to go. See you at the rally." Max hung up just as his door opened.

A smile lit his face. "There's my boy," Max gushed as he rose from his desk.

Jonathan reached out for Max. "Dada," he chanted as he was taken from Harriett's arms.

"Where's Cay?" he asked.

"She had another late meeting with her boss. He has her doing three projects at a time. And you know Cay is going to give it her all," Harriett smiled. "He loves you so much," she said, smiling.

"And I love this little fellow just as much," Max said, lifting him over his head.

"Did Cay say what time she would be getting home?"

Harriett looked at her son with knowing eyes and smiled. "She will be in around eight tonight. She is going to pick the baby up from here. Well, let me get to my desk. The part-time volunteers will be in shortly." Harriett reached for the baby.

"No, Mom, I'll keep him for a bit. I haven't seen him in a while. Right, Little Man?" he cooed.

"Okay, I will have his playpen brought in, if that's okay."

"Yes, that's great." Max sat behind his desk, with the baby on his lap.

When Cayla arrived at the campaign headquarters, the place was abuzz with volunteers answering and talking on the phones. Harriett smiled when Cayla walked in. She was carrying a white bag. "Hello, Cay," Harriett greeted.

"Hi, Ms. Harriett." She returned the smile. "Where's the baby?" she asked.

Harriett had been bringing Jonathan with her to the office whenever Cayla had to work late. Harriett was a godsend. Cayla had offered to get a nanny, but Harriett didn't want any strangers raising *her baby* and nixed that idea quickly. So it worked out fine.

"He's in the office with Max. Go on in," she said.

"I brought something for Max anyway," she said, showing her the white bag.

"I hope it's food. The boy hasn't stopped to eat since this afternoon," Harriett said.

Cayla smiled. "He's going to love this then."

Maxwell's face lit up when he saw Cayla ease open the door. He came from behind his desk. He put his finger to his lips and tilted his head to the side of his office. Jonathan was fast asleep in the playpen.

"Hey, you are a sight for sore eyes," he greeted with a kiss on her cheek.

"Hey yourself," Cay smiled. "I know you're busy, so I won't keep you. Plus, I'm almost brain dead myself. I just came to get the baby and to bring you this," she said, lifting the bag.

"What is it?" he asked, taking the bag from her hand and opening it.

Max opened the bag, and the aroma that hit his senses had him drooling. He grinned at her and set the bag on the small table. He quickly washed his hands and sat at the table.

Cayla grinned when he pulled out two chili dogs and an Orange frosty drink.

"Knowing you, you haven't stopped to eat. So there you go."

Max smiled at her. He stood and kissed her on the lips, surprising both himself and Cay. He sat down before he let his mind regret the small kiss. "Thanks, Cay," he said before he bit into the chili dog.

"You are welcome," she said. "I better get this little boy home." Cay turned to leave.

"Can you sit for a minute?" Max asked.

"Okay." Cay sat across from him. "What's up?"

"Mom tells me you've been working a lot of late nights. Is everything okay at the design firm?" he asked.

"Yes, it's fine. Mr. Dorsett has been loading me up with small projects lately. After I finished those two large projects, he has just been pushing off these smaller, nonessential jobs on me." She sighed. "But it's okay. I'm making a name for myself."

"I don't know why you don't open your own design house. You have the talent - and the experience now. Didn't you tell me you have acquired a small client list?" Max asked.

"Yes, but…"

"No, Cay. You can be your own business. You have the means, baby."

Cay looked at him. "You think I can do this?"

"Cay, you could always do it." Max smiled at her.

"Let me think about it more, okay? I want to ensure my son is not adversely affected." She rose from the chair.

"Never that. You know you can always talk to me about this, right?" Max said as he too rose.

"You worry about the election, Mr. Mayor. We have time to talk about my future, okay?"

Bianca walked into the campaign headquarters. She didn't see Harriett at the desk, and she used the opportunity to walk straight into Max's office located at the back of the room. Whenever that old bat was at the desk, she made her sign in and then she had to wait until she could see if Max was available. Most times, she would leave without seeing him. Other times, she would see him coming out of his office with Avery and Broderick in tow. He would wave and continue talking to them as if she were not even important. She thought she would be in the thick of things for this election, but it had only put a wider wedge between them.

Max and Cayla were looking down at the sleeping Jonathan. "I hate to wake him up. He's going to be so cranky," Cay said.

Max looked at Cay. "You know what? You're a good mom," he said.

Cay melted in his eyes. "Thank you, Max. That means a lot to me," she said softly.

Max leaned forward and kissed her forehead just as the door opened. "What the hell is going on here?" Bianca shrieked.

Max and Cayla turned. The baby jumped and started to cry.

Bianca slammed the door. She stomped past Max and pushed Cayla, staking her claim. She was getting ready to go ghetto central all over this little heffa. Bianca lifted her hand to slap Cayla, and Max stepped between them, glaring at her. "Don't even think about it, Bianca," Max hissed.

"Yeah, Bianca, a black eye and busted lip wouldn't look good on you," Cay said. She turned to her crying baby and lifted him into her arms while cooing to him that everything was okay. She picked up the diaper bag and put it over her shoulder. She then looked at Max. "We'll talk later. Goodnight."

"Dada," Jonathan cried, reaching for Max while Cay opened the door and walked out.

Bianca rolled her eyes and moved to sit in the chair in front of his desk. *Unbelievable. Now the brat was calling him Daddy.*

Max moved to sit behind his desk. "What the hell is your problem, Bianca?"

"My problem? I walk in on you and Cay kissing and you ask me what my problem is?" she shouted.

Max's eyebrows dipped. "You will lower your voice," he barked.

Bianca sucked her teeth, rolled her eyes and folded her arms across her chest.

"What you need to come to terms with Bianca is that Cayla and Jonathan are my family. There is nothing going on between Cay and me. She was my best friend's wife, and I made a promise to be in his son's life and to love him as if he were my own. Either you are going to accept that or we need to rethink this relationship."

Bianca stood and leaned her hands on his desk. "What relationship? The only people who know we have a relationship are you and me. I want all of Atlanta to know we are a couple. I hoped one day we would announce our engagement." Her eyes teared.

Max dropped his head. That was another problem he was now dealing with since he announced his run for office. The women's clubs were questioning him about his marital status. They didn't trust a single man running for office to set a complimentary example for the youth of the city. If he were to get married or even announce an engagement, he might be able to pacify that group of voters. He lifted his head and looked at Bianca. It was something to consider - or was it? He had to speak with Avery soon and get his view of the situation.

Max exhaled and rose from his desk. He pulled Bianca into his arms. Her arms wrapped around his neck. "Bianca, please be patient with me. When the time comes, I will be happy to introduce you to the public as my woman. Let me get over the preliminaries of the election. Then you will be at my side all the way to the Mayor's Mansion."

This seemed to pacify Bianca. She pressed her lips to his, kissing him passionately. When she lifted her head, she smiled at him. "Can I expect you tonight?" she purred.

"Not a good idea, sweets. There are eyes all over me. I don't want the press to get the wrong idea and bash us as being sordid. After we go public, it will be okay for me to visit you. Now, I have to get back to work on this speech for the rally." Max kissed her and walked her to the door.

When Bianca got in her car, she texted Margaret Sherman. *"It time to get rid of that bitch."*

Grant Dorsett studied the finished project plans that Cayla emailed to him. He couldn't help but be impressed with Cayla's work on projects he would normally turn down or refer to another design firm. The software program that she designed was helping her to work faster and accurately. He had suggested that she patent the software because it was a designer's dream. She was on budget, and the clients were pleased with her work. Her designs were damn good. Too bad Bianca had it in for her. Dorsett could only shake his head at the events he knew were sure to unfold.

He had met Bianca when she first arrived in Atlanta, and they have been off and on lovers ever since. Bianca was a talented lady - in the bedroom, the car and even in the elevator. He couldn't get enough of her. Their current arrangement worked for them because they both loved variety. However, she had her eyes on a bigger prize, and that was to become the First Lady of Atlanta. She assured him that her soon-to-be title and husband wouldn't stop them from getting together from time to time to play. Her only request right now was that he keep Cayla busy and out of her way while she worked her magic on Maxwell. Cayla had the last three projects he had given her completed and on his desk way before the deadline. He didn't know what else he could do to keep her busy. Dorsett looked through his files and blindly picked more projects for Cayla Sherman, all for the sake of a piece of nookie. What had he turned into? He just prayed that things would not backfire on him because he didn't want to tangle with the future mayor in no way, shape, form or fashion. Plus, his conscience was beginning to kill him; but oh well, it wouldn't be the first time, he thought.

"Do you have what I need?" Bianca asked the geeky IT tech Peter at her company. Of course, she paid him in the only way that got men to bow down to her. **Good and out of this world sex...**

"When can we get together again," Peter asked, pushing his thick-lensed glasses up his nose.

"We will talk about that later," Bianca said. "What do you have for me?"

He lifted his phone and pressed a few buttons then handed the phone to her to view his work. Bianca slid picture after picture of Cayla in various positions of humiliation. Her favorite was the one where she was sandwiched between two men. Bianca continued to scan through the manipulated photos.

"I found a video someone put on Facebook of a mother slapping her baby in Walmart. The video was grainy but that works for us. She could be this woman you want," Peter explained.

Bianca watched the video. It was grainy, but it could work. When the woman abusing her child looked up at the person videotaping her, it was Cayla's face that

Peter manipulated into the scene as the abuser. She was cursing out the person with the phone. She even grabbed for the phone, but the lady hurried away.

Bianca looked over at Peter. "You are awesome. This is perfect. Send it to me now," she ordered. "Meet me at my place tonight, and I'll have everything you need along with your sweet reward." Bianca smiled seductively at Peter. "See you tonight, lover boy."

When Bianca left Peter, she sent the video to Margaret Sherman with instructions. *Tomorrow while I'm at the rally, go to CPS on Canal Street. Report that you have proof that your ex-daughter-in-law is abusing your grandson and that you need assistance immediately before she kills him. Margaret, you must put on a show. I need tears and hysteria. After your act, show them the video, and I'll take care of the rest.*

An hour later, Bianca was sitting in the office of the Honorable Douglas T. Stratham. The judge was not happy to see her. A year ago, they had a brief affair, but when she started hounding him about leaving his wife of fifteen years for her, he dropped her before she could blink an eye. He hadn't heard from her after she threw a tantrum that night because he wouldn't yield to her demands. So, why was she here now, he wondered?

"What can I do for you, Bianca?" the judge asked.

"Oh, Doug, you don't have a warm greeting for me? I thought we were special friends," she purred as she sat in a chair in front of his desk and crossed her legs, allowing her skirt to slide up to reveal she was butt-naked underneath.

"That was a year ago. What can I do for you? And please respect me enough to pull your damn skirt down!"

"Oh, Doug, don't be like that," she laughed. "I need a tiny favor," she said.

The judge frowned. "What kind of favor, Bianca?"

"I need for you to hold back on a case that will be coming across your desk. You are still presiding over child abuse cases, aren't you?"

"Yes, but I won't do anything illegal for you, Bianca," he stated.

"Oh, you will do this - and it's not illegal. I just need you to hold back the case that is getting ready to be reported. When it comes before you, take the abused child and give him to the grandmother, or I can just go and see Mrs. Stratham and tell her about our hot and heavy affair. Oh, and did I tell you I have a video and pictures of our tryst?" she asked smugly.

The judge's face turned a deep red. "Are you blackmailing me?" he shouted, coming to his feet.

"Oh, Doug, not blackmail. You are just doing a favor for an old friend. I would hate for our little affair to hit social media. You know with all these women reporting sexual harassment by these powerful men. You don't want to be another Harvey or Matt. I think I would make a great spokesperson for the *Me Too Movement*. What do you think?"

Doug sat back down. "Is the child being abused? This isn't one of your plots to remove someone out of your way, is it?" he asked.

"You wound me, Douggie Poo. Of course the child is being abused. I would never make something like that up. I have a video from the grandmother who has witnessed it. You just make sure that the grandmother gets the child." She gave him the mother and the grandmothers names then stood and made her exit.

After she left ole Dougie's office, Bianca was quite pleased with herself. Her friend Margaret will have her grandbaby, and Cayla will be pushed out of Max's life as a known child abuser. Life was good.

Everything was falling into place. *"I am sooo good..."*

Avery and Broderick read the dossier on Bianca Steele that the investigator had delivered earlier. "She has been a very busy and naughty girl," Avery commented, handing the report to Broderick. His eyes quickly scanned the papers.

"Damn, she surely has been," Broderick said, his eyes meeting Avery's. "What are we going to do? This could hurt the campaign if this information falls into the opponent's hands. If Maxwell decides to go ahead with the engagement...."

Avery shook his head. "I know we can't let her derail Max, and we have to protect him. Let's keep a close eye on her until we bring Max into the loop. We don't want a big blowup before the rally, not with the media sniffing around." Broderick nodded his agreement.

"Will she be at the rally tomorrow?" Broderick asked.

"Standing right beside Max, as he requested. She's been complaining that he is not making her known to the public. I think she's broken him down. He's going to start being seen with her." Avery shook his head. "We definitely can't let that happen now, but we have to be careful about managing this. From the report, she's one volatile woman. For now, put some additional female staffers around Max at the rally. That way, Ms. Steele won't stick out too much. Also, don't let her say anything to the press. Cut her off if she tries."

Chapter Fourteen

Cayla had been off work for a few days because Jonathan caught a stomach virus which kept them both up most of the nights. Finally, he succumbed to sleep. Cayla laid him down in his crib and kissed his forehead. She was thankful that his fever had broken.

Harriett had offered to stay with him, but she was called into the campaign headquarters. Since Cayla could work from home, she pushed Harriett out of the door and promised to call her later with an update on Jonathan. Cayla was happy for Max because the rally was a great success, and they were even busier at the headquarters. The polls continued to turn in his favor. Cayla turned on the television and chuckled when she saw highlights of the rally. Bianca was standing beside Max and grinning like she'd won the lottery. She was his girlfriend, and her place was beside him.

Oh, well. Cayla had admitted to herself long ago that she was in love with him. She recognized that Max loved her, but not the way she wanted him to. He was like a big brother, and now that he and Bianca seemed to be getting serious, she couldn't and wouldn't interfere with that. She wouldn't be surprised if they announced their engagement soon. She had survived a lot tougher things in her life. Maybe it was time for her to start dating again. She had been asked out by a couple of the guys at the design firm, but she wasn't interested. Maybe she should start getting interested. After all, she was still a lovely woman. Plus, she still had all of her teeth, she laughed.

Cayla opened her laptop while the baby slept to get some work done on the latest project Dorsett had assigned her. She had only been at it for a few minutes when her doorbell rang. She lifted her phone and looked at the time. It was just a little before noon. Maybe it was Ms. Harriett. She had been calling to see how Jonathan was feeling. Maybe she wanted to see for herself.

She put her phone in her back pocket, went to the door and pulled it open. There was a woman standing there and a police officer with her. "Are you Cayla Sherman?" the woman asked.

"Yes, how may I help you?"

"I'm Mrs. Connelly, supervisor from CPS. May we come in?" she asked.

"CPS? Why are you here?" Cayla questioned while stepping back.

"Is your son Jonathan present, Mrs. Sherman?"

"Yes. Why?"

"Officer, do your duty," Mrs. Connelly ordered the officer before she left the room.

"What's going on here?" Cayla shouted, going after the woman.

"Mrs. Sherman, you need to come with me," the officer said.

"Why?" Cayla questioned.

"There has been an allegation of child abuse levied against you," the officer replied.

"What? I don't abuse my child!" Cayla said and turned to leave when the officer grabbed her. Cayla pulled away from him, but he pulled her back. "What are you doing?" she screamed. She heard Jonathan crying. Cayla moved to go see about her son, but the officer pulled her back again.

"Please don't fight. Just stay calm," he pleaded.

"She's taking my baby, and you want me to be calm? That ain't happening! Now move out of the way and let me check on my son!" she cried.

"She's just doing her job, ma'am. Whenever abuse is reported, we must investigate. So please settle down."

Mrs. Connelly came back to the room with a crying Jon. When he saw his mother, he started reaching for her, but Mrs. Connelly ignored his cries and kept it moving straight out the door. Cayla followed suit with the officer still holding her arm.

"Where are you taking him?" she yelled at the woman.

"I will see you down at the courthouse," she said and put the crying baby in the car seat, while the officer led Cayla to the police cruiser. Cayla sat in the back of the police car with tears streaming down her face.

The police officer took her to the police station and led her to a small room. "Please have a seat. Someone will be here to talk to you soon."

"Where am I going? You people have my baby," she yelled. Cayla knew she had to be calm. She pulled her phone out, sat down, and called Mark Rodgers, her lawyer.

"Hi, Cay, what's up?"

"Mark, they took my baby!" she said.

"Who took your baby?"

"CPS!" she cried.

"Where are you?"

"At the police station near the courthouse."

"I'll be right down."

After hanging up, she called Ms. Harriett.

"Ms. Harriett, I'm at the police station near the courthouse. CPS took my baby." Now she really started to cry. It all started to come down on her. What would she do if they kept her baby?

"Yes, ma'am, I called my lawyer, and he's on his way."

"I'm on the way." Harriett hung up.

Cayla dropped her head and shed more tears of pain and sorrow. She didn't know what was going on, but she would bet her life that Mrs. Sherman was behind this. She had threatened to have her baby taken away. Well, she had to prove it. Now Cayla was pissed to the highest of pisstivity. Well, if Mrs. Sherman wanted a fight, damn it she had one now, and when the dust cleared, she was going to wish she had never crossed Cayla.

After taking the baby, Mrs. Connelly had called Mrs. Sherman and told her she was bringing her grandson to her temporarily, per the written order, until the court case came up.

Mrs. Connelly parked outside the address written on the form for Mrs. Margaret Sherman. She glanced at the baby in the rearview mirror. She didn't know what to do for him except follow the legal documents.

His nose was running, and the poor thing was scared to death. He had cried himself to sleep. However, this was her job. The order said to take the baby to Mrs. Margaret Sherman after he was taken from the mother. Sometimes she hated this job. By the looks of the young woman's home, she didn't look unstable. It was Mrs. Sherman who showed up with the video and her attorney. Mrs. Connelly saw how his mother had slapped the baby when he was sitting in a shopping cart doing nothing. Mrs. Sherman demanded CPS do something. It was her attorney who threatened to have the department investigated and go to the media if they didn't do something. He said it wouldn't look good to report CPS was letting an abused child stay in an abusive home. Her hands were tied, and as supervisor, she did what she had to do, by following orders.

She got out of the car and took the baby from the car seat. She prayed he remained asleep. She sighed when he laid his head on her shoulder. Mrs. Connelly looked up to see Mrs. Sherman standing on the porch and grinning with two younger women.

Mrs. Connelly handed the baby to Margaret. "Look at him, girls. We have our Jon back," she said.

"Mrs. Sherman, I will call you with the date to be in court. You must be there," Mrs. Connelly said.

"We will be there," Margaret said. She then turned and walked into the house with the baby in her arms.

"Where's his mother?" one of the girls asked.

"She was taken in to the police for questioning," she answered.

Both women giggled. "I hope they throw her in prison and lose the key." They too turned and followed their mother into the house. Something didn't set right with Mrs. Connelly as she drove out of the posh neighborhood. There was more than meets the eyes going on here.

Max was in his office discussing strategies with campaign manager Avery, speech writer Everett Somers and debate coach Marvin Combs. They were about to go over the upcoming debate scheduled with Republican Thomas Rashford next month when Max decided to give the team a heads up.

"Before we get started, Avery, I wanted to let you know that I'm going to propose to Bianca," Max said.

Avery wasn't surprised. He saw it coming and was prepared. Now he had to let Max know what he was getting himself into.

"Hold that thought," Avery said as he opened his briefcase and pulled out a folder.

Max frowned at Avery. He looked at the folder in his hand. "I need you to read this before you make that decision."

Just then the door opened, and Harriett rushed in. Max looked at his mother and came to his feet. Tears were in her eyes. "CPS has taken the baby from Cayla," she cried. "She's at the police station now."

Avery went to Harriett. "Calm down, Harriett, and tell us what happened."

"Cayla just called me. She said CPS has taken the baby."

Max headed for the door. "No, Max, you stay here. You can't get involved until we find out what's going on," Avery said.

"That's my godson!" he shouted. Avery stood in front of him.

"Son, think about the election. This could hurt you if there is any truth in it."

"It's not true!" Harriett yelled at Avery.

"I can believe that, but Max has to be careful of the press. They could misconstrue the truth. I'll go down with you, Harriett. We will take care of this. Call Broderick," he said to Max as he and Harriett left the office at a quick pace.

Max stood there looking helpless, pained, and discombobulated. Who would do this?

"I can't do this now," he said to the two other men the room. "Can we pick this up tomorrow, please?"

"Sure, Max. Take care of things here." They left him alone.

Max sat at his desk and gazed out of the window, feeling lost. He needed to be with Cayla to help her with this farce. He knew that his boy was scared. He could feel it. Who could have reported such nonsense? Whoever it was would live to regret it. He would make sure of that.

Cayla stood when Mark rushed into the room. Cayla rushed over to him, crying out, "They got my baby, Mark, and I don't know where he is." Mark hugged her to him.

"Okay, sit here and let me see what's going on." He left the room and went to the desk sergeant. He spoke to the man for some minutes and returned to Cayla, almost ready to give her an update. He had documents in his hand and was still reviewing them when Cayla asked, "What is it?"

Mark let out an agitated sigh. "Someone contacted CPS and accused you of abusing your baby. They say they have a video of you slapping him," Mark said.

"I never laid a hand on my child," she cried.

"Who was the person who took the baby?"

"Mrs. Connelly from CPS. She just walked in my house along with a police officer that had accompanied her. He told me I had to come to the police station with him. Where's my baby?"

"CPS has him. They are not going to tell us where he is until this is cleared up." Mark was now pissed. "That means we have to go to court. Let me make a few calls. We are going to fix this right now."

The door opened, and another officer walked in.

Mark had just hung up the phone. He looked at the officer. "Is my client under arrest?" Mark asked.

"No, sir, we just want to question her about the alleged child abuse."

"As her attorney, that will not be happening today. Until I have looked into the matter, you won't be asking her anything. Is she free to leave?"

"She's not under arrest, but…"

"Thank you," Mark said and led Cayla out of the room.

Harriett and Avery entered the police station. When Harriett saw Cayla, she rushed to her and embraced her with all the love she could muster. "Baby, what's going on?" Harriett asked frantically.

"They took him from me. They took my baby." She fell back into Harriett's arms and sobbed as if her heart had left her body. "Where's your lawyer?" she asked.

"He's talking to someone. He says we have to go to court."

Harriett looked over to see Mark letting whoever was on the phone have the business. He then hung up.

He walked to them, and he was not happy. "This is bullshit," he cursed.

"What's going on?" Cayla asked as she wiped her face.

"We are going to meet with Judge Douglas Stratham in his chambers. He presides over child protection cases. It was his name that was on the order that the desk sergeant gave me. I know the judge well, and I'm sure we can get to the bottom of this." Since Cayla was not under arrest, Mark went to the desk sergeant and told him he was taking his client home.

"Let's go," he ordered. Cayla, Harriett and Avery followed him to the courthouse just a block away.

Judge Stratham nervously paced his office after his call from Mark Rodgers. Mark was a top-notch lawyer with the oldest law firm in the state of Georgia. His name rang from the mountain tops, and now he had set his sights on him. Well, he was not going to put his career on the line for this psycho chick and ruin everything he had accomplished. It had been a couple of days since he had received the papers on Cayla Sherman from CPS. He had instructed Mrs. Connelly to take the baby to the grandmother. He cursed. What the hell had he allowed Bianca to get him involved in? He knew this was some personal shit with her because he knew how much of a witch she could be when things didn't work out in her favor. He had to find a way to bring down Ms. Bianca Steele and get the baby back to Cayla Sherman without this mess hitting the media. Plus, now he had to deal with a respected colleague and ... Shit, Shit, Shit....

Before entering the Judge's chamber, Mark asked the others to wait in the outer office while he went in to speak to the judge alone.

"Please have a seat, Mark," Judge Stratham said.

Mark refused the seat. He slammed the form on the desk. "What the hell is this, Doug?"

"Please, Mark, sit down," Judge Stratham offered again.

"I don't want to sit down. I want you to tell me why you signed an order for the child to be snatched from his mother? I have known you all of my life and have never known you to do something of this magnitude," he yelled.

"Please, Mark, let's talk about this calmly and rationally," the judge implored him.

Mark took a deep breath and sat, when what he really wanted to do was beat his cousin's ass.

The judge cleared his throat. "I'm being blackmailed by a sadistic she-devil and drop the damn formalities. You know you're my cousin and best friend."

Mark frowned, then exhaled. "Okay, but what the hell does that have to do with this baby being taken by your orders, D-Man."

Judge Stratham told Mark about he and Bianca Steele's past, along with her ultimatum.

Mark looked at him with disgust. "I should beat your ass for even messing around on Linda. So, to protect yourself, you would ruin a woman's life by taking her child - all because you couldn't keep *your shit* in your pants. You should have had her arrested on the spot," Mark said.

"I know and I'm sorry. Man, I was scared shitless because all I could see was Linda walking out of the door and not looking back when she received the pictures and videos from Bianca. So yeah, I panicked and bowed down to her wishes. Plus, she claimed she had a video of the child abuse and that CPS would have a copy within the hour. Her main objective was to have the baby given to the grandmother until the court date came around."

"Margaret Sherman," Mark hissed. He knew for sure now there was more to this. "You've been played. Now, how are you going to fix this shit storm that you're in?"

"Well, I am assuming Mrs. Sherman already has the baby in her possession. So, I will rescind the order, have the baby turned back over to his mother and clear her name," the judge told Mark.

"Okay then, that will work. And I want to see this video. The mother is waiting for me in the hall, along with friends. I will drive them over to Mrs. Sherman to pick up little Jonathan."

The judge pressed a few keys on his computer and turned the screen to face Mark. He stood and looked at the grainy video showing a woman slapping her baby and telling him to shut up right there in the Walmart. Mark instantly could see that it wasn't Cayla. The woman was much larger than her, and upon closer inspection, the woman had blonde hair. When the abuser turned to face the person filming her, it was Cayla's face. Mark could only shake his head. "This is a fake. Even you should be able to see that, 'D'," Mark said.

"Yeah, I did take a closer look after she left and realized that I had been suckered."

"Yet you still put in the order," Mark said disgustedly.

"Yes, I did, alright? But I came clean and told Linda about the affair and what this woman was doing to me now - along with an innocent baby. She wasn't happy, to put it mildly. I will be crawling on my knees for a while. Since it happened a while ago, I'm hoping that we can put this behind us. Honestly, I am just praying that she can forgive me and not leave me. I know I made a mess of things. I have to expose Bianca and all of her dirt. I'm hoping I can do so without any media involvement. A person like that usually has a lot of skeletons in her closet."

The judge lifted the phone and called Mrs. Connelly. She affirmed that the baby was with the grandmother.

A few minutes later, Mark left the judge's office with the new order in hand. It was time to shut down this fiasco.

As soon as Mark walked into the outer office, Cayla, Harriett, and Avery were on their feet.

"What's happened?" Cayla asked.

"Where is he?" Harriett asked anxiously.

He held up his hands. "Wait a minute. Wait a minute. Margaret Sherman has him, and we are about to knock on her door and get our boy back. I have the rescinded order. Avery, you drove, I hope."

Avery nodded.

"Well let's go then. We'll talk further on the way."

At headquarters, Max's phone buzzed. Quickly he answered. It was his mother. "Where is my boy?" he asked frantically.

"We are on our way to get him now." Harriett told him what Margaret Sherman had done. Mark had purposely left out Bianca's hand in all of this drama; however, he would fill Avery in on everything when they were alone.

"I want her charged with something, Mother. I'm sick of Mrs. Sherman's mess," Max shouted.

The door to his office opened, and Bianca walked in. She could hear Max shouting on the phone from the hallway.

"Mom, please bring him home and tell Cayla I'll be by to see them after I finish up here." Max was fuming after he hung up the phone. If Mrs. Sherman were a man, he would surly call him out.

"What's happened, Maxwell?" Bianca asked, pretending concern while holding onto his arm.

"Mrs. Sherman went to CPS on Cayla and they took the baby. Can you believe that?" he said.

"What?! Who is this Mrs. Sherman?" she asked.

"She's Cayla's former mother-in-law, and she has given Cayla a hard time ever since she married her son, even after his death. Now she is after the baby. How selfish is that? Instead of trying to help her, all she does is try to find ways to discredit her. Jon is spinning in his grave."

"Oh my God, did she get him?"

"Yes and the judge just rescinded the order. The video Mrs. Sherman had is a fake, and the judge is not pleased. He may bring Mrs. Sherman up on charges for filing a false claim of child abuse. I feel no pity for her."

"I hope Cayla gets him back. I know how much you love that baby," Bianca said with disguised distaste. "Are we going to dinner?" she asked.

"I'm sorry, Bianca. I'm going to wait for word of my son," Max said and turned away to look out the window of his office.

Bianca rolled her eyes. "We can order in, baby. I know you haven't eaten all day."

Bianca went to him and hugged him from behind. "You don't need this kind of stress with the election and all, honey."

"Trust me, if Avery hadn't stopped me, I would have gone down to the courthouse myself."

"Oh, come on, Maxwell. I'm sure that Cayla has everything handled. Is Chinese okay?" she said with a roll of her eyes. *I wonder if this fool realizes that he calls that brat his son. I must get a handle on that before he slips up on TV with that mess, but first things first.*

"I'm going to the ladies' room then I'll call in the food order."

Bianca quickly made a beeline for the ladies' room. She called Margaret, her co-conspirator.

"They are coming to take the baby," she said.

"I thought he was mine until…"

"The order was rescinded. Cayla and her lawyer are on their way to your house as we speak. So you better think of something fast, and if you know like I know, you will not mention my name to anyone. A quick FYI, I know about the parentage of your kids. So, if you don't want me to put you on blast, you best forget you ever met me. *Understood?*"

After Margaret hung up with Bianca, she couldn't believe the nerve of that little bitch. But right now, she had to do whatever she had to in order to keep her baby because she wasn't giving him up willingly.

She frantically called for her daughters to bring Jonathan to her right away. Once they entered the room with Jonathan in tow, Margaret told them that they were coming to take the baby back to that woman.

"Why, Mother? I thought the judge gave you custody of him because of abuse?" Sharon, the older sister, said.

"He took the order back, Sharon. They are on their way to get him," Margaret yelled. She started to pace. "Let me think... Let me think. Oh, what to do? What to do?"

She stopped moving. "I got it. Take the baby and check into a hotel. When they come here, I can honestly tell them I don't have the baby. Now, hurry. You have to go now," Margaret ordered. She all but pushed them out of the door.

"What about his things?" Sherri asked over her shoulder. Both girls were talking at the same time.

"Mom, I don't know about this. We can all go to jail for disobeying a written order," Sharon said, unsure of what to do.

"Just do as I say. I'm not giving my baby back! He's all I have left of your brother, and I will not give him back. I won't! You hear me!" Margaret screamed. "Just get some baby things after you check into the hotel, and I'll call you when they're gone. Now go, girls, go."

Chapter Fifteen

The ride to Margaret Sherman's house was tense. Cayla silently sat in the backseat of the car with Mark, looking out of the window. Her fists were clenched so tight, her knuckles were a shade lighter than her skin. The only thoughts on her mind were getting her baby back and then possibly forgetting that Mrs. Sherman was her elder because she intended to beat the living hell out of her - and anyone else who got in her way. Mrs. Sherman always said Cayla was ghetto, so she intended to show Ms. High and Mighty just how ghetto she could be.

Mark reached over and covered her hands. Her head turned, and she looked at him like a woman ready for battle. The fire he saw blazing in her eyes was not just volatile; he also recognized that if they didn't keep an eye on Cayla, she would tear Margaret Sherman not just one new one but two, and it would be well within her right.

"How in the hell did Margaret get the baby in the first place?" Harriett asked from the front seat.

Avery's eyes met Mark's in the rearview mirror with questions in his blue eyes, seeking answers as well. He wanted to make sure that this little drama didn't leak to the press and jeopardize the election. They had to play it smart because presently Max was the front runner.

"I thought we'd concentrate on getting the baby safely back first and then we could discuss the full situation when we meet up with Max tonight," Mark replied.

Harriett looked back at Mark. Her eyes narrowed. "What's going on, Mark, and don't you dare sugarcoat anything either," she demanded.

Avery reached over and entwined his fingers with hers. She looked at him and then at their joined hands. A warmth she hadn't felt in years moved up her arm.

She eased her hand out of his and folded both hands on her lap. She didn't have time for these feelings at the moment.

"Don't worry, Harriett. We will take care of everything. I promise," he assured her.

"The only thing I want to take care of is beating Margaret's conniving behind. She has gone too far this time, and I mean to put a stop to this immediately," she said, turning her head and looking out the window in a huff.

Margaret watched the luxury car pull into her driveway with some guy behind the wheel and Harriett sitting in the front seat like she was some queen on a throne. She didn't know who he was and didn't care either. But one thing she was sure of was that they were not getting her grandson, under no type of circumstance. Harriett and Cayla didn't wait for the men to open the doors for them. They were out of the car and rushing up the stairs to the large antebellum home before the car was put in park. Before Mark and Avery could catch up with them, Harriett was already banging on the door.

"Open this door right this minute, Margaret," Harriett yelled. "I saw your sneaky behind peeking out of the window."

The door was snatched opened. She glared at Harriett. "Why are you banging on my door like you're the damn police?" Margaret hissed, looking at Harriett like she was something she had stepped in.

"Where's my baby?" Cayla yelled, pushing past Margaret and walking through the house.

Margaret gasped. "How dare you, you-you little…"

"Shut up, Margaret!" Harriett said, getting up in Margaret's face. "You better tell us where the baby is before I forget I am a lady!"

Mark and Avery rushed to the ladies and pulled Harriett back a couple of steps before she started swinging.

"I don't know what you are talking about." Margaret gave Harriett a smug look and turned to walk away.

Harriett reached out to grab the back of her head, but Avery anticipated the move and quickly moved her further back, telling her to cool her jets. They could hear Cayla moving from room to room.

"Mrs. Sherman, I am Mark Rodgers, Cayla's attorney. We have the papers saying that the baby was delivered to you. I suggest you present him or…"

Before Mark could finish his statement, Cayla rushed back into the room. "He's not here," she yelled and was going after Mrs. Sherman, before Mark quickly held her back.

"Like I said, I don't know what you are talking about. You mean to tell me she has lost my grandson? That is so like you, Cayla," she self-righteously replied.

Harriett pulled out of Avery's arms, and he quickly pulled her back to him.

Mark was across the room quietly talking to Cayla. "You need to stay calm. We've got the law on our side. Let me handle this," he told her. "Please." Cayla nodded.

Avery was still talking to Harriett and trying to keep her calm, but it was a hard task.

"Now, let's start again, Mrs. Sherman." Mark pulled a legal document from his inside pocket. "A Mrs. Connelly from CPS brought Jonathan to this house under false claims that you made against Cayla, which have now been reversed. If you don't present the baby in the next five minutes, you will be arrested for kidnapping and filing a false claim, which could give you fifteen to life in prison."

"I don't have him. She never brought him to me, I swear it. Now you people get the hell out of my house, right now!" she shouted.

Harriett had enough. She pulled away from Avery. He reached out to stop her. She gave him a look that told him, *touch me and you will lose that arm.* Avery dropped his arm and silently began to pray as Harriett quickly approached Margaret, who had the good sense to take a step back.

"You want to play this little game, Margaret, huh? Well let me tell you how this little game of yours is going to play out. If you don't have Jonathan here in the next five minutes, I will have to let everyone know that you have a few things you don't want known. Now you think hard about what you are doing, because I can hear the bones in your closet rattling to be freed. You got me?"

Harriett stared at her. Margaret's heart leaped. *No, she didn't know about that. She couldn't know,* she thought.

Margaret rolled her eyes. "I don't have him," she repeated. "And I already told you I have no clue what you are talking about."

"You must think I'm playing with you. So let's take a walk down memory lane, shall we, my dear? Now, I know how you are about your social status and appearances. God knows you think you are some grand lady and a pillar of elite society. It would be sad if everyone began hearing the rumors that the son you claimed to be Jonathan Sherman Senior's didn't have one iota of his DNA. And I am not too certain that the others you claim to be his don't fall into that "non-DNA" category as well." Harriett gave a dry chuckle. "So, I will advise you again not to test me or I will let the *bones* fall where they may."

Margaret's eyes widened and she gasped as her hand went to her chest. "How…"

"You don't think I knew you were cattin' around with my cousin Jules before you married Jon Sr.? When you found yourself in the family way, you lied to Jon and told him that he was going to be a father. He did the noble thing and married you to save his family from the scandal of you having his child out of wedlock. But don't get things mixed up, he was happy about the baby; he just wasn't happy about having to marry you. It's obvious that cousin Jules had it going on because you kept going back to him over and over, and this makes me wonder if your daughters are his as well. So yes, you married into one of the wealthiest black families in Atlanta back then, but my family knew all of your dirty little secrets."

Harriett shook her head sadly and tsked. "For Jon Jr.'s sake, I thank God he and Jon Sr. never figured out your deceit because they would have been mortified. Now, I suggest you hand over the baby, or everybody in our little elite group will know that Margaret Sherman is a fraud, adulterer, and a liar."

Margaret's face paled. Her lips moved but nothing was coming out. It looked as if she was about to pass out in a heap.

Cayla and Mark were stunned beyond belief. Avery dropped his head to keep from laughing at the look on Mrs. Sherman's face. Oh yeah, he thought. His soon-to-be lady had beauty, spunk, and fire – just plain feisty as hell.

Harriett stood looking at Margaret with her hands on her hips. "Now, this is the last time I'm asking you: where is the baby?"

Margaret moved to the house phone sitting on the side table and dialed. "Bring the baby back," she ordered and hung up the phone in defeat.

Cayla let out a relieved sigh and leaned against Mark.

Margaret looked like she had aged ten years in just a matter of minutes. She sat down heavily on the sofa with her head down, while the others remained standing. She looked back up at Cayla.

"I want to see my grandson," she whined.

"That's not likely to happen now, Mrs. Sherman. If you had come correct, I would have considered it, but now…" Cayla turned away from her.

"You do realize, Mrs. Sherman, had you held out on the whereabouts of the child, I could have had you and your accomplices prosecuted. I still might do so, the more I think about it," Mark snapped.

"Please, I-I'm sorry. I was desperate. She would have never let me…"

Harriett sucked her teeth. "Shut up, Margaret. I, for one, don't feel sorry for you. You have been doing your dirt to people for years without any conscience. And the way you treated Cayla when she married your son was disgraceful. You know what they say: what goes around comes around. Well, the hens have come home to roost. I suggest you seek therapy." Harriett moved to stand beside Avery. She took his hand in hers.

A door was heard opening. Sharon and Sherri rushed in from the back door, asking questions. "Whose car is that? What happened, Mother?" Sherri said as she came into the living room. The others could hear the baby crying inconsolably. Cayla rushed over and pulled her son from Sharon.

The two stunned women stared, looking at the people in the room. "Mother?"

"Let's go," Mark replied. Cayla held her baby close as she, Avery, Harriett and Mark walked out of the house, not bothering to look back.

Margaret stood and ran after them. "Mr. Rodgers, Mr. Rodgers," she frantically called after him. "Are you going to prosecute me?"

Mark stopped and turned to wait for her. "That's not up to me, Mrs. Sherman," he said and got into the back of the car. He hoped that he would not have to see Mrs. Sherman and her spawns again anytime soon. After dropping the ladies off at Cayla's, Avery drove Mark downtown and quickly returned to Harriett and Cayla.

Bianca watched as Max paced back and forth, and it was getting on her last nerve. He was so tense he couldn't eat the food when it arrived. She tried to distract him with talk of their budding relationship and their promising future together after he won the election; however, her talk of them being Atlanta's new power couple only proved to make him more aggravated.

"Max, please, can't you sit down already? You act as if you are this baby's biological dad. I hope that your calling him *your son* doesn't slip out of your mouth during any interviews," Bianca said irritably.

"What is your problem? Why would you let some mess like that come out of your mouth? You don't have to be here, Bianca. Feel free to leave at any time," he snapped. Max started to think that he had made a grave mistake in considering taking them public. He had to rethink this thing with her because he wasn't sure she was the one he wanted to take with him on his political journey.

Bianca didn't know when to shut up. She continued to throw pot shots at Max. "All I'm saying is that CPS wouldn't have taken the baby without good reason or proof of abuse. Maybe this Mrs. Sherman knows something even you don't know about Cayla. After all, you're not with her 24/7, and isn't she from the ghetto? You know sometimes those kinds of people never change," Bianca said, looking at her nails while thinking it was time for a refill. She couldn't be caught slipping in the beauty department because appearance was everything for the future Mrs. Mayor.

Max stopped pacing to look at her. "What the hell did you say? Are you crazy or what?" Max shouted.

"I'm just being realistic. I think you need to separate yourself from the situation until it is rectified. You don't want it to harm the campaign and your stellar reputation. And it's not as if it's our problem anyway."

"When it comes to my son, I could give less than a damn about this campaign. He comes first, and you better remember that, and don't you ever say anything like that to me again. Am. I. Clear?" Max's eyes had turned to slits before he turned away. "Yeah, this woman has a few screws loose," he muttered. *I have got to handle her, but I have to calm down before I forget I am a gentleman. Please, Lord, help me to hold my mule, as Nonna would say.*

"Max, I am concerned for the baby's safety as well. I want to know if he is alive and well, but my main concern is you," she whined. Plus, she needed to know what happened at the Sherman's residence. She just hoped Margaret heeded her warning and kept her name out of her mouth.

Before Max could lay into Bianca, his phone rang. He quickly answered the phone.

"Mom," he said.

"Thank God it's over," he breathed.

"I'm on my way," he said, rushing out of the office and not giving Bianca a second thought.

"Max, where are you going?" Bianca cried, following him.

"My son is home. I'm going to see him." He didn't stop walking.

When Bianca pushed through the outer door, Max was already pulling out of the parking lot. She rushed to her car to follow him. She already knew he was heading to that heffa's house. But Cayla could bet her sweet ass that she was not getting her man. She just hoped that she didn't have to put her six feet under. She had done it before….

Bianca pushed Mrs. Sherman's number on her car's Bluetooth. The phone went to voicemail. "If that old bat opened her mouth, she isn't going to know what hit her when I'm done with her," she hissed.

Max was driving so fast that she had lost her. That was fine; she knew the directions to his destination.

Bianca pulled up to the curb outside of Cayla's house. Max's car was in the driveway along with another car. She banged on the steering wheel and screamed. *Damn! Damn! Damn!* Things were not going her way. She had to get rid of Cayla and that brat now rather than later. She sat in her car to get control of her emotions. *She had to play the part....*

Max entered the house. His eyes instantly went to the baby in his mother's arms. He almost ran to them. Jonathan lifted his head from Cayla's shoulder. "Dada," he cried and reached for him. Max quickly took the baby from Cayla's arms and hugged him. He looked at Cayla with tears wavering in his eyes. At that very moment, Max realized something very important. He would be lost without Cayla and this baby in his life. He reached out his arm and Cayla walked to him. His arm closed around her. He rested his head on hers and closed his eyes as he held Cayla and the baby close to his heart.

Harriett smiled up at Avery, but he was frowning. "Why is he with that Bianca maniac if he is clearly in love with Cayla?" Avery whispered.

"Stupid," Harriett said with a roll of her eyes.

Suddenly, there was a knock at the door. Max and Cay didn't budge. Harriett went to answer the door. She sucked her teeth when she saw Bianca standing there. "Oh, here comes the drama," she muttered.

"Bianca."

"Is Max here?" she said without even acknowledging Harriett at all.

"Didn't you see his car?" Harriett said, stepping aside and allowing her entry.

Bianca looked at Avery, and the look from his icy blue eyes made her inwardly shiver. What was that look for, she wondered? Whatever!

Her eyes then went to Max with his arms still around Cayla and the baby. He seemed oblivious to her presence.

"Max!" she snapped.

He lifted his head and looked at her.

"Bianca, what are you doing here?" he asked, looking over at her and frowning.

Cayla stepped back. "I'm going to give him a bath and put him down for the night," she said and took the baby. Max kissed him before she left the room.

"Bianca?" Max said.

"I'm just as concerned about the baby as you are, Max. You know that," she said, going to stand beside him.

Harriett rolled her eyes. "Anyone hungry?" she asked.

Max smiled at his mother. "I could eat something, Mom. It seems I forgot to eat today," he said.

"I'll help you," Avery offered.

When they left the room, Max turned to Bianca. "Truthfully, why are you here?" he repeated, moving away from her.

"What were you doing with your arms around that woman? Need I remind you that we are in a relationship, Maxwell? Is this the kind of disrespect that you think I will accept from you? Well, if you think I roll that way, you are mistaken, so you need to get it together, Max, because I am not the one," she snapped.

"Yeah," Max said blandly. "Maybe we rushed into this relationship for all the wrong reasons. I'm finding that you have a lack of compassion toward anyone but yourself. And I have not forgotten that little statement you made about *ghetto people*, as you call them. Those are the people that will help me get into office, and I will never turn my back on them or anyone else in this city. I will be in the problem-solving business and…" he paused, frustrated. "Never mind. I just don't know if we have a shot at making this work. So feel free to leave, you feeling me, Bianca?"

"So, you are just going to throw me and what we shared away?" she asked incredulously.

Max let out an exhausted sigh. "At this point, Bianca, there is no 'us', and I don't know if there ever will be. I shouldn't have let it go on as far as it has." His head lowered, and he squeezed at the tension that was creeping down the back of his neck. "I just don't know. Let's talk later. I'm exhausted and in need of food."

Bianca's face reddened, and she was seething. She just *knew* he wasn't dismissing her!

"Oh no you don't, Max. You have been ignoring me. Since the campaign started, we barely see each other. I thought we were in this together. If it's not the campaign, it's Cayla and the baby. I thought we were moving forward with our relationship. You said we were going to go public," she argued.

Max shook his head. "See, there you go with your mess. I said we will talk later, and that is what I meant," he growled.

"Come have a sandwich, Max," Harriett called from the kitchen.

Max walked away without another word.

Bianca cursed under her breath. "Don't bet on it, Max. There will always be an 'us'."

Cayla leaned over and kissed her exhausted baby. She turned the baby monitor up on the night stand and left the room with the second one in her hand. Bianca was standing in her living room alone. Why was this wench still in her house? She stopped and looked at her. She hadn't forgotten that she had stepped to her once before. Let her try that mess this time. It will be on and popping.

"Bianca, where is everyone?" she asked.

"In the kitchen," she snapped. Cayla turned to join them.

"Cayla," she called. Cayla stopped and faced her.

"Max is mine," she hissed.

"And what is your point?" Cayla asked.

"I'm going to be his wife, and you need to come to terms with that. He can't keep running to your rescue whenever you are in trouble."

"I'm not trying to come between you and Max. What you need to do is learn to accept that he is going to be in my son's life. I am no threat to you."

Bianca changed her position. "You're right. What was I thinking? He loves that baby very much, not you. I'm sorry if I came off wrong to you."

Cayla shrugged. "Whatever."

"Can I use your bathroom?" Bianca asked.

"Sure," she said and joined the others.

Bianca's eyes narrowed on her back. Does that tramp think she's stupid? She's using that baby to try and break us up. She was no one's fool. Instead of going to the bathroom, she slipped to the back of the house and inside the baby's nursery. She stood beside his crib, glaring down at him.

Cayla stood in the archway, which lead into the kitchen. Max and Avery were sitting at the table, eating sandwiches and talking. Avery was telling Max that they were going to meet Mark down at campaign headquarters and that they had something very important to discuss with him.

"How's my baby?" Harriett asked, smiling at Cay.

"He's out like a light," she said, setting the baby monitor down.

Harriett smiled. "Eat something, baby," she said to Cayla. She leaned into Cayla. "Did Bianca leave?"

"No, she's using the bathroom. She's a trip," Cay said. "She told me Max was hers and that she was going to be Max's wife," she told Harriett. "I guess that was supposed to set me straight."

"Max is not going to marry her. Soon he will see her for the witch she truly is." Harriet interjected.

Cayla frowned and looked at the monitor.

"You better eat, honey," Harriett said.

Cay paused and then stilled. "Shh," she said and picked up the monitor. She motioned for Harriett to follow her.

"You little brat, I'll be damn if you are going to come between me and Max. After he marries me, I got plans for your little ass. So your momma better pack your little ass up and go away if she knows what's good for you and her, and that's a fact. I will not be playing step momma to you. It be so easy to lift this pillow." Bianca whispered, although her voice could be heard clearly through the monitor.

The two ladies exchanged astonished looks. Cayla handed the monitor to Harriett. She walked up behind her and grabbed a handful of her hair. Bianca screamed as Cayla drug her out of the nursery. In the living room, Bianca pushed Cayla away from her. The baby was awakened by Bianca's screams, which scared him and caused him to start crying.

Bianca stumbled back, looking outraged. "What's your damn problem!" she screamed.

Harriett went into the nursery to see about the baby. Max and Avery rushed into the living room just in time to see Cayla start doing her thing with Bianca.

"Didn't I tell you that you wouldn't look good with a black eye and bloody nose? Well let me prove my theory to you." Cayla swung and her fist landed in Bianca's face. *Pop.*

"Cayla!" Max yelled, but Avery pulled him back. "What are you doing?!"

Bianca's head snapped back. "Oh no you didn't, bitch!" Bianca screamed and swung back. She missed and Cayla's fist landed two more times in her face. She fell back against the mantel and fell to the floor. Bianca grabbed her face, screaming. Avery went and grabbed Cayla while Max went to Bianca.

Cayla yelled struggling to get to her.

She looked up at Max and shouted. "She attacked me for no reason, Max." Her hand covered her eye as blood trickled from her nose.

Cayla pulled away from Avery. "It wasn't for no reason, you liar! I heard you tell my son that when you married Max, you had plans for his little ass - and that I had better pack his ass up and go away. "This trick said a pillow would be so easy. What plans did you have, Bianca, huh?!" Cay yelled. "Let me tell you something. I will waste you if you ever step to my son again, you sorry heffa."

Max helped Bianca to her feet. "I didn't say that," Bianca moaned up at Max.

"Trick, I heard you on the baby monitor. Your crazy behind snuck in my baby's room like he would know what you were saying." Cayla looked over at Max.

"Get her out of my house, Max," Cayla yelled. "If that is what your choice in a wife is, more power to you. But you best keep her away from me and my son, and if you can't, then you stay the hell away from him too!" Cayla gave Bianca another hard look before she left the room. "Don't forget what I said, Bianca, because I meant every damn word."

Max was confused. He looked at Bianca. "I swear I didn't say any such thing, Max. She's crazy. She just attacked me for no reason at all."

Max shook his head. "Go home, Bianca. I'll talk to you later."

"What are you going to do about this? I'm going to have her bought up on charges," she screeched.

Max led her to the door. "Go home, Bianca! I told you we were through anyway. You had no reason to come here unannounced," Max snapped.

Bianca snatched away from him. "You believe her?" she asked incredulously. "I've invested too much time into you, Maxwell, so I *will* be speaking with you later. You just can't throw me away like some old shoe. Damn you…"

Harriett came out of the room. "If he doesn't believe Cayla, then he's a fool. I heard it too. Now call me a liar," Harriett said.

Max's head turned sharply to look at his mother then back at Bianca. "Go home, *NOW,* Bianca!" He opened the door. She gave him one last look and walked out the house.

"Mom, what the hell is going on in my life?" he asked.

"And it ain't over yet, son," Avery said. "We've got to meet with Mark and Broderick. Let's go."

Avery looked over at Harriett. He walked over to her. She looked up at him. He leaned close to her and whispered. "Damn woman, you are amazing. That was so hot." He kissed her on her cheek then turned and followed Max out of the house.

Chapter Sixteen

Max sat silently in the passenger's seat and replayed in his head all that had transpired, as Avery drove them to campaign headquarters. His son was taken by a desperate, vindictive, bitter woman; then, Cayla attacked the woman he had contemplated taking as his wife. He had stopped thinking of making Bianca his wife after he accepted the fact that he was in love with Cayla. What kind of marriage would he have had when his heart belonged to someone else? He knew he loved Cayla, that he did not doubt, but she was still in love with her husband, wasn't she? He felt all kinds of guilt about it. *Take care of Cayla and my son,* Jon had said in his dream. Then he was gone.

Did that mean he was free to fall in love with her; make her his own? He was exactly what his mother said: stupid.

"You okay, son?" Avery asked.

Max looked over at him. "I'm not sure yet."

"Well, I know this much: everything will be made clear once we've spoken to Mark and Broderick," Avery replied. There was a pregnant pause.

"Maxwell, may I ask you a personal question?" Avery said.

The corner of Max's mouth lifted. "Depends on how personal."

"Oh, I'm gonna get all up in your business," Avery chuckled.

Max laughed - not at the statement in general but at Avery's use of slang. "Hey, you are my campaign manager. Go ahead and get all up in my business."

Avery glanced at him before focusing on the road. "What in the hell do you see in Bianca, other than the obvious?"

"Obvious?"

"Yes, obvious. I'm a man, and I can see that she is a beautiful woman, educated, even sexy - and probably very skilled. However, that's outer packaging.

I can also see that she is manipulative, evil and very calculating. She's the type of woman that will stop at nothing to get what she wants."

Max rolled his eyes. "Get to the point, Avery," he barked.

"Do you love her?"

That was easy for Max to answer. "No."

Avery's head turned sharply and he frowned. "Then why are you with her?"

Max let out a sigh. "She started out being a distraction. I even parted with her for a while. But like you said, if Bianca wants something, she doesn't stop until she gets it. Nevertheless, I already told her at the house that we are through."

"I see. And you are right, she will get what she wants, and by any means necessary," Avery muttered.

"What?"

"Listen, I consider myself a fairly intelligent man - and pretty astute. You say you used Bianca as a distraction. Well, I'm here to tell you it's not working. Every time Cayla and the baby come within your vicinity, your love for them shines in your eyes like a beacon. Son, don't you know you can't hide true love?"

Max opened his mouth to protest. Avery shook his head. "I know you love your godson, but you also love his mother. You can't hide it. What is it your mother says you are?"

"Stupid," they both said in unison, then they laughed.

"Neither of you understand why I shouldn't love Cayla."

The conversation stopped when Avery pulled into the lot of the headquarters. It was late, and all the workers and volunteers were now gone. Mark and Broderick were standing at the door, anxious to get the meeting started.

Dorsett had his eyes closed and his hand fisted in the hair of a beautiful redhead as she took him in her mouth with great skill and precision. His eyes popped open when he heard the banging on his door and the frantic ringing of his bell. "Go*t*damnit!" he cursed.

He rolled the beauty off of him and sat on the side of the bed. He glanced over at the pouting naked beauty. "Hold that thought, beautiful. I'll be right back. He grabbed the back of her head and kissed her hard on the mouth. He then lifted his phone and looked at the security camera. The person at his door had her back to the camera, but he knew that body anywhere. He cursed then snatched his robe off the clothes tree and put it on.

Dorsett bounced down the stairs, aggravated. He snatched open the door.

"What the hell?" he growled.

Bianca pushed him out of the way. Dorsett watched as she paced his floor, cursing in English and Spanish.

Bianca stopped to look at him. Dorsett's eyes widened. It looked like Bianca got her ass beat. Both of her eyes were blackened, and one side of her lip was split, swollen and had dried blood.

"I hope you don't have company, Dorsett," she snapped.

"As a matter of fact, I do, so we will have to talk about this…"

"Hell no!" she interrupted. "I need you." She turned and trotted up his stairs. When Dorsett realized her intent, he followed.

The redhead was in the center of his bed when the door was flung open. She quickly paled and pulled the sheet up to cover her nudity.

Bianca looked around the room at her scattered clothes on the floor. She lifted them and tossed them to the scared woman. "Get out!" Bianca shouted.

The redhead looked at Dorsett. "You stay," he said. "Bianca, you are the one leaving." He glared at her.

Bianca went to the bed and grabbed the woman by her hair and began to pull her from the bed. The woman was screaming and grabbed Bianca's arm. Dorsett snatched Bianca away and tossed her against the wall.

The redhead got out of the bed and started to dress. "That bitch is crazy, and I don't need this drama," she screamed as she quickly pulled her dress over her head and stomped out of the bedroom.

Bianca stood with her legs astride and a smug smile on her bruised face.

Dorsett's eyes narrowed. "I should slap the daylights out of you, but it looks as if someone else already has. What did you do now, Bianca? Looks like you messed with the wrong person this time," Dorsett chuckled.

"Go to hell, Dorsett!" Bianca screamed. "I want you to fire that bitch Cayla!"

Dorsett frowned then he laughed. "Don't tell me sweet little Cayla did this to you?"

"Damn it, you are my friend, and I want you to fire her now, Dorsett. But you better trust and believe that I will get her."

Dorsett stopped laughing. "Let's get something straight, Bianca. You don't tell me what to do, and I will not fire her. She's the best up-and-coming designer that I have, and I thank you for bringing her to me. Plus, I like, respect and admire Cayla. Now you can walk out of here or I will throw you out. Better yet, why don't I call Cayla and have her do it for me," he laughed.

Bianca gasped. "How can you talk to me like that?" she yelled.

"I can because I will not get involved with your manipulating bullshit. Cayla's a good person and excellent designer. You just stepped on the wrong toes and over-played your hand." Dorsett went to her, grabbed her by the arm and led her out of his house. Before he closed the door in her face, he said, "Go get you face fixed." Then, he slammed the door.

Max sat at the round table in his office and looked at the faces of the men surrounding him. Whatever was going on, it was serious. Avery cleared his throat. "Do you have that dossier I gave you before everything happened this morning?"

"Yes," Max rose from the table and went to his desk. He pulled out the folder he had placed in the drawer and placed it on the table. He then retook his seat.

"Max, as you know, we had to vet everyone that was involved with you for your protection and the protection of the campaign," Broderick said.

"Yes, I know that." Max looked confused.

"Well, we had to vet Bianca Steele and discovered a number of red flags. I know that you were thinking of proposing to Ms. Steele, but I'm going to advise you to hold off until you have read the dossier."

"Red flags? What the hell is going on?" Max roared. He was so tired. He just wanted this day to end.

"Just read the file, son," Avery said.

Max opened the file, and his eyes moved over the papers as he quickly turned page after page. He wasn't a quarter way through, when he closed the file and looked up at the men, looking dumbfounded. He pushed out of the chair and stood, turning his back on the others. He rubbed his hand over the top of his head. Bianca was an embezzler and manipulator. She blackmailed people in the last company she worked for just to be at the top of the corporate chain. There were even reports of affairs that caused many men to lose not only their families but their jobs as well over the years. She wasn't even who she claimed to be. Her birth name was Rosalina Rosario. Her parents' nationalities were Puerto Rican and African American, and she was from the Bronx in New York. Everything about her was a lie. Anger seared through Max's body. He turned sharply and looked at the men before him, men he trusted. "I'm going to assume by the looks on your faces there is more," Max said through clenched teeth.

"Just recently, the PI that we had investigating her went to the design firm where Cayla Sherman works. He had gone there to speak to Grant Dorsett. The receptionist was away from her desk, so he walked back to the sitting area and took a seat. Since he wasn't announced, Dorsett didn't realize he was even there, and the door to his office was ajar. The PI said it was purely coincidental what he stumbled upon. He was there to speak to Mr. Dorsett about Mrs. Sherman when he came upon this." Broderick pressed a few buttons and handed Max his phone.

Dorsett had Bianca lying face down across his desk, and he was banging her like there was no tomorrow. Max had seen enough and handed the phone back to Broderick. He sat heavily in the chair and pinched the bridge of his nose.

"Mark, please tell me Bianca was not involved with the taking of my son," he said lowly.

Mark sighed. "Wish I could, man. The only way that I know of her involvement is that my cousin, Judge Douglas Stratham, was being blackmailed by her." Mark told him how she went about her little scheme.

"She said she didn't know Mrs. Sherman," Max said.

"Well, we all know that isn't true now. I could kill my cousin for his part in this. However, he did reverse the order, and Cayla's name has been cleared of those allegations. You can thank your mother for handling Margaret Sherman. Now what we have to decide is what to do about the attempted kidnapping of your son…"

"And, what to do about Bianca," Avery added.

"Right now I want to kill them both and bury them in the Georgia woods, but that would not look good for a man running for office," Max said. "I'm angry as hell right now, gentlemen. I think I should delay those decisions until my anger has abated and murder is no longer on my mind. But just so all of you know, I wasn't taking my relationship with Bianca to the next level. I had already called it quits, but thanks for the support." Max pushed away from the table. "I need to get out of here for a while." He then walked out of the building.

Avery and the others exchanged looks. "Is he alright to be alone?" Broderick asked, concerned.

"Max is a levelheaded man. He'll be fine," Avery said.

Max pulled up to his destination and sat thinking for a minute before leaving the car. He stood a few feet away and just looked at the headstone. He reached his friend and stooped down. He wiped his hand across his name. He smiled a sad smile.

"Hey, man, I know it's been a minute since I've come to visit, but I have so much drama, confusion, and guilt going on in my life that it's unreal. I need your counsel, man. Nobody else can help me but you. You were always my "ears" and could always pull me through whatever pain I was enduring." He dropped his head. "Damn, man, I—I miss you so much…."

"Right now I need you to hear me and let me explain this guilt that has me wondering about my sanity. I've fallen for your lady. I know. I know. Remember you came to me in a dream and told me to take care of Cay and your son? Well, that caring has turned to something much stronger. I love her, man," he finally admitted. "It didn't start out that way. She just captured my heart with her genuine kindness and sweet ways." Max chuckled through his tears. "But, Dogg, when she smiles at me, my entire world lights up; and when she says everything is going to work out, hell man, I believe it. And, Jon, you should see Little Man. He is awesome. When I hold him, all I see is a mini you. Then he smiles up at me, and all is right in my world. Man, it makes me feel invincible."

His tears were now a steady stream. When he finally got himself together, he wiped the wetness from his face. He then picked the conversation back up with his best friend. "I almost forgot. I am running for Mayor of Atlanta. I know. You told me I would make a great politician one day, and Mom is beside herself. She doesn't like the lady I was dating. You know it must be bad if Mom put her out the house. I don't need to say anymore." Max laughed. Oddly, he was feeling better now that he was releasing some of the stress.

"I know who I want to be my First Lady, but I am so reluctant because I don't want to disrespect you. I wasn't trying to step into your shoes; I don't want to, but, man, damn....Look, Jon, give me a sign that it's okay. Make the wind blow; knock down a tree; hell, make a cat meow or something." He laughed again. "Real talk though, I'm so torn. Even though I know that you'd understand, I still had to "man up" and come tell you about it. I love you so much, man, and miss you like crazy. I'll be back soon," he promised.

Max stood, walked back to his car and got inside. He gave one last glance at Jon's resting place before driving off. He drove through the street aimlessly until he realized he had driven around the block several times. A calmness had now settled over his heart. He took a deep breath and exhaled. That is, until the Bluetooth in his car beeped. *"Call from Bianca Steele,"* it said.

Max rubbed his hand down his face. *Just when you think things are going to be fine, the devil always shows up.* The anger had eased came back in a hurry, just at hearing her name. He was going to ignore it, but then decided against it. He pressed the button on the steering wheel.

"What do you want, Bianca?" he barked.

"Maxwell," she whined. "You need to do something about Cayla. I have two black eyes and my lips are split."

"Bianca, now is not the time for me to talk to you, but believe me, it will be soon - that I promise you."

"You believe what that heffa said about me?" she snapped.

"You need to be glad Avery pulled her off you. She had every right after what you did, and yes, I do believe her. As a matter of fact, you have a lot of nerve to even call me after you threatened my son. You didn't think I didn't hear Cayla say, you said a pillow would be easy. I know you are a deranged woman now and I'm done talking."

"Max! Max! Please listen to me. You love me," she shouted desperately.

"Bianca, I never loved you, as I told you earlier. We are finished." Max hit the button that ended the call.

Max laughed dryly. He *was* stupid. He looked in his rearview mirror and made a U-turn in the road. He didn't stop until he was parked outside Cayla's home with the engine running. He looked at the house. The living room light was still on which meant Cayla was still up. He smiled when he remembered when she first moved in. At first sight, she'd loved the house he had chosen for her. She was heavy with her son then. For him, those were the happiest times he and Cayla had shared. Max rested his head on the headrest and closed his eyes.

"Call from Bianca Steele," was announced on the Bluetooth again. He ignored the call, turned off the car, and went to see Cayla. He had to let her know that she had become his heart.

He went to the door and rang the bell. Max stood there with hands deep in his pockets and waited for her to answer the door. After a minute, the door opened.

"Max, is everything alright?" Cayla asked.

"Yes, everything is fine. May I come in?" he asked.

She glared at him. "I thought you would be with your intended, nursing her wounds," she said sarcastically.

"No," he said and dropped his head in shame, especially now that he knew all that he knew.

He lifted his eyes and met hers. "Please, may I come in?"

Cayla stepped aside and let him pass. She closed the door and stubbornly folded her arms across her chest.

"What do you want, Max?" she asked.

"How's my boy?" he asked first.

The air rushed out of her, and her body seemed to deflate. "He's been waking up and screaming every few minutes. I think he's been traumatized, Max. When I pick him up, he wraps his little arms around my neck as tight as he can. I just put him down." Tears filled her eyes.

"May I see him?" he asked. Cayla nodded and followed him into the nursery.

Jonathan was sitting up in the bed, his little face wet. He saw Max. "Dada," he whined and lifted his arms to him. Max lifted the baby and held him tight.

"What's up, Little Man? I'm here. You don't have to be afraid anymore." Max's heart was breaking at the sight of his little face. He walked to the rocking chair and sat down then cradled Jonathan in his arms and rocked him as he talked softly to the little boy that was looking up at him. Cayla laid her hand on Max's shoulder. "You hungry?" she whispered.

"I could eat something," he said as he watched the baby.

Cayla left the two of them alone.

Max continued to watch the baby as he rocked him. "I will never let anyone hurt you ever again, Jon. I will take care of you and your mom to the best of my ability. Nothing will ever touch you again. *This I promise."* His voice was soft. Jonathan lifted his little hand and touched Max's lips. Max kissed it. "I love you, Son."

He continued to rock him until Jonathan's eyes closed. Max eased from the rocking chair and gently took him to the crib. He kissed his forehead softly before he laid him down and covered him with his favorite blanket. He turned the nightlight on and the overhead light off, leaving the door opened. He found Cayla sitting at the kitchen table with her head down and shoulders shaking as she silently cried. Max moved to her side and stooped down beside her chair. Her head lifted as she met his eyes.

"Baby, I'm so sorry for everything," he said. He reached up and wiped a tear from her eyes with his finger.

"Max, I was just sitting here thinking. What if we hadn't figured out where they had taken my baby?"

"Then we would have moved hell or high water to find him." Max stood up. "He's sleeping now. I think he will stay down tonight." He moved and sat at the table.

"Your mom fried some chicken and made potato salad before she left," Cayla said. She got up to serve him.

"You sit; I'll get it." Max rose and went to the fridge. He pulled out the two items and set them on the table.

While Max ate, Cayla watched him. "What happened to Bianca?" she asked.

"I don't know. I had a meeting with Avery, Mark and my PR guy. The meeting was very enlightening." Max went on to tell her what he had learned about Bianca. He waited to tell her about Bianca's part in the taking of Jonathan. Max got silent. Cayla frowned at him.

"What aren't you telling me, Maxwell?" she asked.

Max exhaled and put his fork down before wiping his mouth with his napkin. "Bianca was behind Margaret getting the baby."

"What? How? I didn't even know she knew Mrs. Sherman," Cayla said.

Without going into detail, Max summed up how Bianca and Margaret were in cahoots together.

Cayla shook her head. "I guess evil attracts evil," she said and stood up from the table. Max watched her leave the kitchen. He cleared the table before he joined her. She was sitting on the sofa with her legs folded under her. Her head was back, and her eyes were closed.

She had been through it today as well.

"Cay," Max called softly.

She lifted her head. Cayla looked at him and could see his face etched with sorrow. His eyes were filled with apology and an echo of pain.

"If you can forgive me, I promise you that nothing like this will ever happen again," he said and turned to leave. Cayla rose from the sofa.

Max stood with his hand on the door knob and his head down. Suddenly he turned to face her. His strong features were tight with determination.

He walked away from the door with long strides and stopped in front of her. He grabbed her arms, and she looked up at him inquiringly. "Damnit, Cayla, I can't anymore," he said huskily.

"You can't what, Max?" Cayla asked.

"I can't deny the way I feel about you any longer. Even before Little Man was born, I loved you. You remember the time we made love?" he asked. He moved his hands down her arms and took her hands in his.

Cayla nodded. She had never forgotten those magical moments.

"I felt so guilty. All I could think about was that I made love to my best friend's wife, and the guilt ate at me. However, I now know what Jon would say about me, you and Little Man. He came to me in a dream and said, *"Tell my son about me, Max. Tell him I love him very much, and that I will always be watching over him. Max, just remember there is only love. Fill your life with it while you can. I know it won't be easy. There are obstacles you and Cay will have to get over, but I truly believe that Cay will complete you. And if you love her as I feel you can, it will be easy. Love her, Max, with all your heart."*

"I do, Cay. I do love you with all my heart. I have for a very long time. I'm ashamed now to say I used Bianca as a distraction to keep me from pouring my heart out to you when I knew you still loved Jon. Bianca nearly destroyed us, and that is my fault. For that, I beg your forgiveness."

Cayla looked up at him with tears wavering in her eyes. "I loved Jon very much, you knew that. I didn't think I would love like that ever again. And like you, I felt guilty after we made love. But you are not Jon. You are Maxwell Washington, the most gentle, loving man that I know. You are a true man who loves his best friend's son as if he were his own. Jon will always hold a special place in my heart, but I love *you*, Max. I have for a very long time. Then I saw you with Bianca one day, coming out of the Ritz in Buckhead. That is when I let all hope of you loving me go." She lowered her head.

Max dropped her hands and gently cupped her face in his large hands. "You love me?" he asked, stunned.

"I'm afraid so, very much." She gave him a watery smile.

Max's head lowered, and he captured her mouth as if he were a starving man. Cayla lifted on her toes then wound her arms around his neck and kissed him as if she were also starved. Max's arms held her tightly. She lifted her head and looked in his eyes.

"Would I be too forward if I said, *make love to me, Maxwell*?"

Max grinned at her and lifted her from her feet. Cayla giggled and wrapped her arms around his neck. In the bedroom, he gently laid her on the bed. Both fully clothed, Max lay beside her and they looked into each other's eyes. Cayla began to unbutton his shirt. Max lifted the t-shirt she wore over her head.

One by one, their garments fell until they were both naked and gazing at each other. The feel of her skin jolted his senses. Max pulled her into him and covered her mouth with his. Cayla felt his heated hardness press against her belly and she moaned. Max rolled to his back, and he filled his hands with her butt as their mouths melded together in heated wild kisses. His tongue warred with hers, invading her mouth with a wet heat. She was the first to end the kissing, as her mouth nibbled on his hot skin and worked its way down. Max grunted when her mouth sucked at his nipple. He sank his hands in her thick hair as she moved down his strong muscular body. Cayla came up on her knees and looked at him with lust-dazed eyes. He was all sleek muscles and chiseled to perfection.

"You are one fine man, Maxwell Washington," she purred. She scraped her nails lightly down the hard muscles in his abdomen. Her head lowered and she kissed his tip before she licked the great length of his manhood. Max moaned and rolled his head on the pillow. When her mouth closed over his heated flesh, he strained his body and mind, fighting the rush that built within him. He reached down and easily lifted her, making him pop from her mouth. Max then laid Cayla beneath him.

"Oh no, baby, this is not going to end before it starts," he panted. He went in for the kill and covered her treasure with his mouth. *Pay back, darlin'.* He was leaving nothing out. His mouth sucked and licked. When his tongue pushed inside her, Cayla arched as pleasure racked her body. She was trapped between torment and ecstasy as she exploded. Max rose above her as her body withered, and he grinned. "You ready?" he whispered against her mouth. He then pushed her knees up and lay between her smooth thighs. *"Have mercy,"* he hissed. *She's so fine.* His shaft teased her entrance, rubbing without entering as her folds coated him with her wetness. "Umph," he grunted.

Cayla's eyes opened. "Don't tease me, Max. Handle your business - now!" she breathlessly replied.

Emboldened by her own reckless desire, she lifted her hips, and the tip of him slipped into her silky heat. With just a small move of his hips, Max plunged deep into the sweetest heat imaginable. Her burning hotness gripped him. They froze after their bodies were united as one. Max and Cayla gazed at each other; they couldn't believe that they were finally together. He pressed harder into her. Deeper and deeper he went until he filled her up with his maleness. She was deliciously tight, and her walls tightened around his manhood as he filled her to completion. Cay rotated her hips in slow circles around his rigid instrument. It wasn't long before she was meeting his driving rhythm. He rode her body hard with the passion of the beast. Faces close, fingers entwined, they moved to the raw rhythm. Her damp heat stoked him and held him prisoner within her scorching walls. Her muscles gripped him tighter and tighter while pleasure racked her body with each firm thrust. They made sounds without words, only noises of pure primal pleasure. The sound of sweat-slicked skin slapping filled the room. Together they gasped, moaned and writhed.

Again Max had to fight the sensation and struggled to hold on just a little longer. The need to explode built within him like a rising crescendo as the buzz of sexual heat built between her legs. A shock of pleasure possessed Cayla, short circuiting her as erotic oblivion gripped her. Max body jerked hard and every muscle tightened. They gasped, groaned and gave into mutual pleasure as the power of their orgasms sent them into shivering ecstasy. They both careened over the edge and came to a mutual surrender.

Reluctantly, Max rolled off Cayla and lay back with pleasure-glazed eyes, staring at the ceiling in wonder. They lay quietly panting in their afterglow. When Max found the energy to speak, he rolled his head on the pillow and looked at her in amazement. All he could say was, "just... wow." No woman had ever felt so good, so perfect. Cayla rolled her head to meet his gaze and smiled.

"Just... wow," Cayla echoed.

Max grinned with pure male satisfaction.

Cayla scooted closer and lay on his chest with her head tucked under his chin. Max kissed her temple before they dozed, wrapped together in the blissful afterglow of satisfaction.

Chapter Seventeen

Cayla went back to her bedroom with Jonathan following behind her in the walker. She moved over to the bed and looked down at the sleeping man that had rocked her world throughout the night.

"Just... wow," she whispered.

He had his arm thrown over his head, and the sheet covered his lower half. He was one fine man, she thought.

She lifted Jon out of the walker and sat him on Max's chest.

"Dada," he giggled as he bounced on his chest.

Max's eyes fluttered open. "Morning, Little Man." His voice was gruff from sleep as he lifted Jon in the air, causing him to squeal. Max glanced over at Cayla and smiled. "Morning."

"Morning to you too," she smiled. "I've made breakfast, and I left things in the bathroom for you." She took the baby from him so he could get up. He got up naked and made his way to the bathroom.

"Um-um-um," Cayla muttered, before leaving the room.

A few minutes later, Max joined her and Jonathan in the kitchen. The baby was in his highchair with a spoon in his hand and banging on the tray as his mother fed him. Max had his phone in his hand.

Max leaned around the baby's head and kissed her on the lips. "Thanks for last night," he said before he kissed her again.

"My pleasure," she murmured. "Your phone has been buzzing constantly."

Max sat down and looked at the ten missed calls and voicemails. "Please finish feeding him while I fix you a plate," she said as she moved from the chair.

Max laid the phone down and began to feed the baby. He didn't want to think right now about the people that had blown up his phone. He also didn't want to think about what was ahead for him. He just wanted to enjoy these precious moments. He had the rest of the day to deal with the chaos that had become his life.

He looked at Cayla as she scrambled him some eggs at the stove. "How are you feeling?" he asked.

She glanced up at him as she put the eggs on a plate and added bacon and toast.

"What are you really asking me, Max?" she countered when she set the plate in front of him.

"I guess I'm hoping you don't regret what happened last night," he said before he dropped his head to bless his food.

"Regret? No. However, I know that Bianca is not going to go away quietly. What I want to do is have Bianca and Mrs. Sherman arrested for what they did."

"And we can do that, if that is what you want to do in order to have peace of mind. But I will deal with Bianca first, and you can have the rest of her when I'm finished. She will regret the day that she crossed me and this family," Max said though clenched teeth.

Cayla looked into his eyes for a minute before she moved to tend to Jonathan. She lifted him. "Then take care of your business," she said before walking out of the kitchen.

Max ate his breakfast as he scanned down the list of missed calls and voicemails. He had two from Avery. He was inquiring if he was alright. The other eight were from Bianca. He listened to one of her voicemails, which demanded that he see her; the others, he ignored. "Oh yes, Bianca, we will be meeting today for the last time in your life," he muttered. He made arrangements to meet Avery, Broderick, Mark, and if needed, Judge Stratham. His main objective was to get rid of Bianca, and he had an offer she couldn't possibly refuse. Max finished his breakfast. He could hear Jon and Cayla's laughter coming from the nursery. He leaned against the doorjamb, watching them. This will be his family soon because this is where his heart is. Nothing and nobody was going to stop him from claiming them. The house phone rang. Cayla turned to answer, but Max beat her to it. "Don't worry; I'll get it, sweetheart."

Max answered the phone. "Hello," he said.

"Maxwell," his mother replied, relieved.

"Hey, Mom. Everything alright?"

"Avery was very concerned about you after your meeting. He tried to call but you didn't answer," she said.

"Mom, everything is fine now."

"Why are you answering Cayla's phone?" she asked.

"She's dressing the baby. I was getting ready to go home. I stayed last night, and Cay and I talked," he said, smiling.

"Well, it's about darn time. I hope you got it right this time, Son."

"I think I did. I love her, Mom," he admitted.

"I was beginning to wonder about you, Maxwell - bringing that mess up in my house," she chuckled. "How's the baby? I know he was restless yesterday."

"He's fine. And if you must know, I was beginning to question my own sanity."

"Okay, well since you've figured it out, I'm going to go. Tell Cayla to bring the baby by the house."

"Okay, I will."

"Dada," Jonathan called. He took the baby from her arms. He looked at her. God, he loved her.

"I have a few meetings today. I wanted to take you to dinner, but I won't be done until late. I want us to spend more time together."

"Max, I know you are busy, so when you get done, come here and we can eat together," Cayla offered.

"It won't be too late?"

Cayla leaned up and kissed him then took the baby. "It's fine; just get going. I have a feeling it's going to be a long day."

"Yes, I'm sure you're right. I'll see you later." He kissed her and the baby before she walked him to the door.

Later at his office, Max took a deep breath and called Bianca. *It was time.* He tried to keep the anger out of his voice. Inwardly, he wanted to strangle the life out of her, but she wasn't worth the jail time. He put the call on the speaker and leaned back in his chair when her phone rang.

"Maxwell, where have you been? I have been calling you all damn night and day," she admonished.

"Good morning, Bianca," he replied.

"I needed you," she whined. "You should have been with me after that witch attacked me."

"Be careful, Bianca. You are in no position to make demands. You threatened a sweet innocent child, and I can't have that. You were dead wrong."

"I tell you I didn't," she lied. "Cayla misunderstood me."

"My mother did too, huh?"

"Your mother doesn't like me, Max."

"I think she has good reason. Let's not forget how you acted the first time you met her. You don't know my mother like I do. She takes no mess from anyone. Her dislike of you is on you. Now, I would like for you to meet me at headquarters. We have a lot to discuss, Bianca. Be here by 1pm and don't be late."

"Maxwell…" she called. However, Max had already hung up.

Avery, Broderick and Mark arrived a half hour before Bianca. They took a seat at the table to discuss the position that Bianca could put them in if they didn't stop her in her tracks right now. "What's the game plan?" Avery asked.

"I think she and Mrs. Sherman should be charged," Mark said with disgust in his tone.

"Yeah, we could do that. However, Mrs. Sherman will be going down by herself because it will be Bianca's word against Margaret's," Max said with thought.

"We could always bring the judge in," Mark replied.

"Yes, that is true, but with their arrests, they will point the press to Max. I think we should handle this as quietly as possible," Broderick put in.

"Anyway, I think Harriett got Mrs. Sherman straight. She's worried as hell about her social status," Avery said. Mark and Avery chuckled.

Max's eyebrows dipped. "What did my mother do?"

Avery and Mark told him how Harriett got Mrs. Sherman to hand over the baby.

Max was stunned. "So Jon was my second cousin. Wow. Seems Mrs. Sherman has been the pot calling the kettle black, huh? Mom always said Mrs. Sherman had better leave Cayla alone because she knew some things on Mrs. Sherman that she wouldn't want made public. I never paid it any mind."

"So what are we going to do about Bianca?" Avery asked.

"She is going to leave the state. I figure with all that I've read in the dossier, she has no choice but to abide by our demands or face legal prosecution. Oh, I expect her to argue. She had aspirations of becoming First Lady of Atlanta. And to think I was foolishly going to grant her wish. Thank God I woke up before it was too late." Max shook his head.

"Yes, that was a close call, my boy," Avery chuckled.

The door opened and Bianca walked in like she owned the place, stopping in the doorway and arrogantly looking around the office before becoming perturbed. Max looked at his watch. None of the men greeted her.

"What are they doing here?" she hissed as she walked toward Max. She leaned in to kiss him, but he just walked away and sat behind his desk.

"Have a seat, Bianca," Max said with a wave of his hand.

Bianca stood for a second in the silent room. She rolled her eyes, took a seat in the chair in front of Max's desk and crossed her legs.

"Max, how are we going to talk privately with them here? I thought you had come to your senses about dissolving our relationship," she said irately and loud enough for all to hear.

"Because, these men here have my back, and what we are about to discuss concerns them in an indirect way."

Bianca's pretty little eyebrows dipped in confusion. "I will not talk about our private business in front of them." She stood up. Max rose as well. He went to the chair she'd vacated and turned it to face the three men who wore smug-looking expressions.

"I advise you to sit down!" Max barked.

Bianca gasped and sat down in the chair, stunned.

Max cleared his throat. He looked over at the men at the table. "Broderick, would you like to tell us what you found when you vetted Ms. Steele?"

"Gladly," Broderick said. He began to read off the more serious disclosures listed in the dossier. After he finished, he looked at Bianca whose face was bright red. "Those are some of the more serious activities. The other items disclosed were just relative to her getting what she wanted, and obviously she didn't care who she stepped on to get them. Now I haven't contacted the company you were accused of embezzling from, since you were found not guilty, but the information contained in the public records seem pretty convincing to me. I guess you found a way to get out of that as well."

She looked at Max. "Those are all lies, Max, I swear it," she declared.

"No, Ms. Steele. I have contacted most of those involved. They were more than happy to talk about the illustrious Bianca Steele. They are not very fond of you, I can tell you that," Broderick finished.

Max looked at her with repugnance. "Bianca, I want you to pay particular attention while Mark speaks. It's all yours, Mark." Maxwell moved back to the other side of the large office. He had to move. If he were within arm's length, he wasn't sure what he would do.

Mark stood. "Yesterday, my client was falsely accused of abusing her child and that child was taken away from its mother," he said, sounding like he was in court. "It was later determined that said allegations were false. Thankfully, mother and child have been reunited. The question I asked myself was who would to such a thing? After a small investigation and speaking to the judge that signed the order, I learned that a Mrs. Margaret Sherman made those false claims, and the child was taken to her. But wait, she also had an accomplice." Mark paused and looked at Bianca.

"Why are you looking at me?" Bianca blurted out, coming to her feet. "I don't know Mrs. Sherman," she yelled.

"Make yourself comfortable, Ms. Steele. We will get back to that. Now it was the judge that made everything clear to me. And after we viewed the bad editing job on the false video, he was quick to rescind the order."

"What has that got to do with me?" she snapped.

"You see, that judge - I know very well, and he told me about your attempt at blackmail."

Bianca's eyes widened in surprise, but she quickly covered it. "I don't know what you are talking about," she said stubbornly.

"Judge Stratham, you there?" Mark said.

"Yes. Bianca, don't tell me you don't remember coming to my office and asking me to sign the papers to have the child taken from his parent when Margaret Sherman's complaint crossed my desk?" he asked.

Bianca's mouth dropped open, and the color left her face. She looked over at Max and then quickly dropped her head.

"Thank you, Judge," Mark said and disconnected.

"Ms. Steele, I have two options here. I could press charges against you as an accomplice to Mrs. Sherman or let Max handle this little situation you find yourself in." Mark took his seat.

She again came to her feet quickly. "You won't press charges because it's my word against this Mrs. Sherman's, and I still say I don't know her," she replied cockily.

Mark shrugged. "If you want to go with that. But Mrs. Sherman was singing like a canary and volunteered to put her statement in writing when I told her she could be arrested for making false statements and kidnapping. She told us it was all your plan because of your 'connection,'" he said with air quotes. Mark just put that little tidbit in for good measure.

Bianca gasped.

Max moved from the back of the room. Avery was surprised at how composed he was. He came to stop in front of Bianca and looked into her eyes. He stuffed his hands in his pocket for extra assurance that he wouldn't strangle her.

"Bianca, let me tell you how this little scenario is going to be played. You will leave this state and never return. If I ever see you again, you are going to wish that I hadn't. I blame myself for overlooking your obsessions, your rudeness, and your manipulations. You crossed the line though when you turned your viciousness on my family. I should have kicked you to the curb months ago. I even consider…" Max paused. He looked at Broderick. "You still have that video?"

Broderick unlocked his phone and searched for what he knew Max was talking about then handed the phone to him.

He pressed *play* and then turned the phone to face Bianca. Bianca gasped and tried to snatch the phone from him. Max sneered at her. "And you wanted to be the First Lady of Atlanta. What a joke." He turned away from her with revulsion.

"Max…"

"Shut up, Bianca. I don't want to hear anything from you. All I want is for you to leave Atlanta and never return, am I clear?"

Bianca being Bianca, she placed her hands on her hips, tilted her head and looked Max from his feet to his head.

"Do you really think you can get rid of me that easily, Maxwell, huh?" She chuckled. "Let *me* tell *you*, gentlemen, how this is going to work. And when I get done, you will be asking me how high to jump. For you see, I have inside info that the press would love to print on the self-righteous Maxwell Washington. They have been looking for any dirt that I have, even if I have to make it up. I'll start with you having an affair with that bitch you put on the pedestal. How does this sound, boys: Maxwell Washington, candidate for mayor, was in an illicit affair with his dead best friend's wife." She smiled. "And that's just for starters."

Broderick stood and moved to the other side of Bianca. She looked at him smugly. He looked at Max. "Let me handle this one, Max," he said.

"Well, Ms. Steele. If you feel that way, then let me enlighten you. It seems there is another embezzling case that you were recently implicated in, at your last worksite where you were promoted to VP. Our sources tell us the former CEO, who you blackmailed, is also singing like a canary. He's been charged with embezzling millions from the company and recently named you as his partner in crime. I suspect the Feds will be coming to Atlanta for a visit any day now. So go ahead and give your lies to the press. Right beside it will be the mug shot of you with the caption reading: Bianca Steele, VP of Global Inc, arrested for embezzling millions from home office in Ohio."

"That's a lie!" she screamed.

Broderick pulled out his phone and unlocked it. "Shall I call and confirm the charges?" Broderick lifted a smug eyebrow. "Oh, and Ms. Steele, we have plenty more. However, we will keep that under wraps until you try to pull our hand, then we will bring out the rest of the smoking guns – *Ms. Rosario*."

Her eyes narrowed at each man. "Oh alright already...damn. I'll leave town, and all of you bastards can go to hell," she snapped and headed for the door.

Max stepped in front of her. "I want you gone tonight. And if you don't, I will know." Max stepped out of the way and opened the door.

Bianca stepped out the door. She was defeated and she knew it. Every word Broderick said was true, and she had no choice but to run if the law had been brought in on that Ohio situation. She turned and looked at Max with tears wavering in her eyes. "Max, I…"

"Leave town tonight!" He slammed the door in her face.

Max faced the other men in the room, and he was fuming.

Avery chuckled. "Well done, men."

"Put the PI on her. Tell him to watch her and let us know if she doesn't appear to be preparing to move," Max ordered.

"No worries. He has never stopped watching her. He is probably following her as we speak," Broderick announced proudly.

Max took a seat at his desk. "Now, gentlemen, can we get back to my campaign because I'm going to take this thing."

"Now that's what I'm talking about," Avery said enthusiastically.

After a small discussion about what to do with Mrs. Sherman, Mark bid the others a great day and left.

"Okay, let's get back on the plans for the debate," Avery advised.

Bianca jumped in her car, spoke the address into the navigation and sped out of the parking lot, causing several cars to blow their horns at her.

"Yeah, I might have to leave this country dump, but not before I put something on Mrs. Sherman's ass. That bitch thought I was playing with her. Call Margaret Sherman," she said to the Bluetooth in her car. She listened at the ringing of the phone until voicemail clicked on. She stabbed at the button on her steering wheel to disconnect and cursed violently.

She sped onto I-75 at top speed as she cursed Max and anyone else involved with him. She took the off-ramp at top speed and without yielding to traffic. Many horns blared behind her. She turned off the interstate to the avenue then sped recklessly to the road leading into the wealthy historical community. She called Margaret again. "You better answer this phone!" she screamed in the car. When the call again went to voicemail, Bianca accelerated angrily on the road that was free of other cars. Not knowing the road, she came up on a sharp curve. She pressed both feet to the brakes, and she fought with the steering wheel to veer away from the large tree that stood on the side of the road. The car missed slamming into the tree but not the electrical pole near it. She hit it head-on so hard that the pole broke and landed on the hood of the car, leaving things a jumbled, smashed-up mess.

The PI, who had difficulty keeping up with her, stopped just as Bianca's car hit the pole. Seconds later, the car burst into flames. He called 911 to report the accident. While reporting, he attempted to get closer, but the heat kept him at bay.

Plus, there were live wires all over the ground. He was sure that the person known as Bianca Steele was no more.

It wasn't long before the first responders were on the scene. He told the police what he had witnessed and the estimated speed at which she was traveling. Minutes later, the electrical trucks arrived and took control of the live wires after the fire was completely out. After answering the police's questions, the PI shook his head as he walked back to his car. Before turning and driving away, he called Broderick Matthews.

When Broderick hung up with the PI, he announced, "Bianca Steele, according to the PI who just witnessed everything, was killed on impact when her car drove at top speed into an electrical pole and burst into flames."

"Oh my God," Max murmured. He was stunned and said a silent prayer for her. He wanted her out of their lives but not like this.

Chapter Eighteen

Max hadn't gone to his own home but rather to Cayla's. It was well after nine o'clock, but he had to hold her. He was mentally exhausted. He had spoken to Cayla to tell her that it was too late to come by and that he would speak to her on the next day; however, she was not hearing it. She told him to come by anyway because she wanted to make sure he ate something. Jonathan was spending the night with Max's mother. The only disappointment was that he wouldn't see his boy tonight, because he needed them both. He stood at the door as he waited for Cayla to answer. Bianca is now dead and he's truly sorry about that, but it didn't change the way he felt about her deceit. He admitted that he was hurt and a little humiliated because he hadn't suspected a thing.

The door opened. Cayla smiled at him and stepped aside to let him enter. Her smile faded when she noticed the exhaustion on his face. After closing and locking the door, she went to him. He had his back to her, and he rubbed his hand over the top of his head. Cayla knew that move well. He was having a hard time mentally.

"Can I get you something, Max?" she asked softly.

Max turned. "A kiss and a drink would be awesome, and in that order, please," he said with a small lift of his lips.

Cayla smiled. Just the sound of his voice gut-kicked her. Instantly, she remembered the way he'd made love to her. Her body was responding in a way that meant she would love for him to rock her world again, but something was off. She would wait until he was ready to get it off of his chest. She let out a sigh and walked into his arms. Max looked down into her eyes, and it set his heart to pounding. His greatest desire was to be with her and to enjoy the love they shared. Flashes of their lovemaking had him instantly needing her. However, he needed to let her know what had transpired today.

Cayla looked up at him as a glazed look of consternation began to spread over his face. She knew then that something serious had happened today.

"Max?" she whispered with concern in her tone.

Max gently cupped her face as he continued to gaze into her eyes. His mouth then covered hers. Cayla's hands slid over his strong broad shoulders, and she accepted the heat that came from his mouth. She accepted it in all its glory. He didn't raise his head until he felt that she was thoroughly kissed.

After a quick peck on his lips, Cayla went to the curio cabinet in the room where she stored the liquor and poured him a drink. Max had sat down with his head down. She went to him and handed him the amber liquid.

He smiled at her. "Sit down, baby," he said, patting the empty space beside him.

Max tipped the glass to his lips and threw the drink down his throat, then he placed the empty glass on the coffee table.

Cayla's eyebrows rose. That can't be good, she thought to herself.

Max lifted the hand she had on her lap and brought it to his lips. "Cayla, I have something to tell you, but I'm not sure how to go about it," he admitted.

"Just tell me, Max," she said.

Max took a deep breath before he spoke. He told Cayla what had occurred today. He left nothing out as he conveyed the conversation with Bianca.

"At least now we don't have to worry about her conniving behind," Cayla commented.

"I know," he said," but there is more. Bianca was killed instantly after her car hit an electrical pole."

Cayla gasped and covered her mouth.

"I know. I was stunned as well. It is all behind us now. I don't want to talk or think any longer about the day I had. I just need your loving, baby."

"Well, I suggest you take me to bed and make love to me until you no longer have to think."

And that was exactly what Max did. He made love to Cayla until the sun peeked over the horizon and well into the afternoon.

The next day, Max took a much-needed break from campaigning, deciding he needed more family time. He needed to be around the people he loved to distraction and who would never lie and deceive him. He and Cayla arrived at Harriett Washington's house later in the afternoon. When Harriett opened the door, they could hear Jon babbling and quickly moving across the wood in his walker to join Harriett in the foyer. When he saw them, he cried out enthusiastically. "Dada," he chanted.

They came inside, and Max kissed his mother's cheek in passing directly to the baby. Harriett looked at Cayla, grinning. "Are you the reason my son looks less stressed?"

Cayla's face heated. She smiled and kissed Harriett's other cheek, not answering. She just followed Max and the laughing baby into the living room.

Harriett let out a breath. "Thank you, Jesus," she said, smiling.

Max was lying on the floor with the baby lifted above him. Cayla and Harriett sat together, watching how much those two boys loved each other. While they played, Cayla told Harriett what Max had relayed to her. Harriett shook her head and said she was sorry about Bianca's death.

Max stood with the baby and sat down across from the ladies with Jon on his lap. They discussed the situation briefly and then dropped it. He sat the baby down on the floor and rose. As the grownups talked, Jon, unnoticed, crawled to the coffee table and pulled himself up.

"I need to run a quick errand," Max announced.

Harriett frowned and Cayla nodded. "You *will* be back for dinner, won't you?" his mother asked.

"Yes, Mom, I will." He went to kiss Cayla and then headed out of the room.

"Dada," Jon called out. He let go of the table, and with his little chubby arms out, he took his first wobbly steps to Max, giggling before he fell on his little padded butt.

Cayla and Harriett laughed, while Max looked down at him - stunned. "He walked," he declared happily. He reached down and scooped him up into a hug.

Finally, Max left to take care of the errand, and now with the baby down for a nap, Cayla and Harriett talked while they prepared dinner. Harriett told Cayla that Margaret had come to see her.

"Really? She had the nerve to come over here after what she attempted to do?" Cayla said with attitude. "What did she want?"

"She practically begged me not to tell about the parentage of Jonathan. She swore she would not bother you again but still had the nerve to ask me to convince you to let her see the baby. I told her that I was not going to convince you to allow it, because I sure as heck wouldn't."

Cay shook her head. "She better be happy I'm not going to press charges. I can't see her going to prison at her age. If I did allow her to see Jon, how could I ever trust her not to run off with the baby after the stunt she and Bianca pulled? So no, that will never happen."

"I know you can't, honey," Harriett said sadly. "Margaret did this to herself, and I have no sympathy for her whatsoever. And if it means anything, I think you have made the correct decision."

Later, Avery arrived, just minutes after Max returned. Lately, Avery had been keeping company with Harriett. Max and Cayla glanced at each other. They knew something was developing between them. They knew because whenever Avery spoke to Harriett, the color rose in her cheeks.

After dinner, Max, Cayla and the baby left to return to Cayla's house. Avery stayed for dessert.

Once they were back at Cayla's home, Max bathed the baby and put him down for the night. Cayla was surfing through Netflix for a movie they could watch when Max joined her. He took the remote from her hand and then turned off the television.

Cayla looked at him. "I thought we were going to watch *Black Panther* before going to bed," Cayla replied, looking confused.

"Yes, and we will, but I need to talk to you first." He took her hands. She tuned to face him.

"Cay, you have been through so much this past year, and if I could change any of it, I would do just that to make sure you were happy each and every day. You were my best friend's wife, and I witnessed firsthand the love you and Jonathan shared. However, Jon is now gone and will always and forever be in my heart. I know you told me you love me, and those words were the best thing I have every heard in my life. Now I am hoping you love me enough to become my wife. I promise you all the love I have inside me belongs to you and Jonathan. Please marry me, Cay, and I will make you the happiest woman in the world; this, I promise." Max exhaled a shaky breath. He reached into his pocket and pulled out a black velvet case and opened it.

Cayla gasped when she saw the contents of the box. Inside it was a large pink oval-cut diamond; smaller diamonds surrounded the large gem. Her hand was pressed to her rapidly beating heart. Words failed her. She nodded and lifted her hand to Max as happy tears flowed from her eyes.

Cayla threw herself into his arms, finally able to speak. "Yes, I will marry you. I love you so much, and I can't wait to become Mrs. Maxwell Washington and the First Lady of Atlanta." Max's arms held her tightly. His eyes closed, and he gave thanks to the good Lord above for bringing Cayla into his life.

Epilogue

Three months later, Max and Cayla were joined in holy matrimony in a grand ceremony with all of Atlanta looking on. Afterwards, Maxwell Washington took the oath of office as the new Mayor of Atlanta. There was news media from across the country televising the youngest Mayor to ever hold the office in Georgia. Both ceremonies were held at his alma mater, Morehouse College. The swearing-in event was over-crowded with voters and well-wishers cheering the new mayor on. Mr. Avery Chambers, the campaign manager, proudly stepped to the podium following Max's oath of office and introduced to the country Mayor Maxwell Washington and First Lady Cayla Washington. In Max's arms was his adopted son, Jonathan Sherman-Washington. The new mayor and family proudly waved to the crowd of well-wishers, whom he would serve with dignity, integrity, and honor. He glanced over at his beautiful new bride, with respect and pride glimmering in his eyes. Most importantly, he would love Cayla Washington with every fiber of his being. *Yes, Jon, you were right. She is easy to love. We will all make you proud.*

Made in the USA
Monee, IL
12 March 2022